DEEP DOO-DOO

MICHAEL DELANEY

PUFFIN BOOKS

PUFFIN BOOKS
Published by the Penguin Group
Penguin Putnam Inc., 375 Hudson Street, New York, New York 10014, U.S.A.
Penguin Books Ltd, 27 Wrights Lane, London W8 5TZ, England
Penguin Books Australia Ltd, Ringwood, Victoria, Australia
Penguin Books Canada Ltd, 10 Alcorn Avenue, Toronto, Ontario, Canada M4V 3B2
Penguin Books (N.Z.) Ltd, 182-190 Wairau Road, Auckland 10, New Zealand

Penguin Books Ltd, Registered Offices: Harmondsworth, Middlesex, England

First published in the United States of America by Dutton Children's Books,
a division of Penguin Books USA Inc. 1996
Published by Puffin Books,
a member of Penguin Putnam Books for Young Readers, 1998

10 9 8 7 6 5 4

THE LIBRARY OF CONGRESS HAS CATALOGED THE DUTTON EDITION AS FOLLOWS:
Delaney, M. C. (Michael Clark)
Deep doo-doo / Michael Delaney.—1st ed.
  p.   cm.
Summary: When they discover the power of the transmitter they built,
eleven-year-old Bennet and his best friend, Pete, send out television broadcasts
using Pete's dog to challenge the current governor in his bid for reelection.
ISBN 0-525-45647-3 (hc)
[1. Politics, practical—Fiction.   2. Television broadcasting—Fiction.
3. Family life—Fiction.]   I. Title.
PZ7.D37319De 1996 [Fic]—dc20 96-15136 CIP AC

Puffin Books ISBN 0-14-038747-1

Printed in the United States of America

For Christine

Contents

DEEP DOO-DOO

The Governor's Race

The Ordways were like many families all across America. They lived in a modest house that was in a crowded but friendly neighborhood; they owned two cars—a Ford station wagon and a little Honda sedan; and, at night, they ate their dinner in front of the TV set. Like many families, the Ordways watched the TV news during dinner. On this particular evening, as on many recent evenings, the big news story was the governor's race. This was understandable: It was late fall; election day was only weeks away.

"Oh, come on!" cried Mr. Ordway as, eyes fixed upon the TV screen, he buttered a slice of Italian bread. "Can't you talk about anything else but family values? What about unemployment? What about the state deficit?"

Bennet, his son, looked over at the little TV set that sat on a stand beside the kitchen table. The governor, a tall, handsome man in glasses, stood in front of a colossal American flag, speaking to a group of young schoolchildren—or "youngsters," as he called them.

"Some family values!" scoffed Mrs. Ordway, twirling her fork in the spaghetti that was on her plate. "If he cares so much about families, why did he cut education funding?"

"Talk about real issues!" said Mr. Ordway, addressing the TV set as though the governor could actually hear him.

"Wh-wh-why doesn't he talk about real issues?" asked Bennet, who was twelve years old and had a tendency to stutter. As usual, Bennet was wearing his Boston Red Sox cap. He wore the baseball cap all the time—even during dinner.

"He doesn't want to talk about them," said his mother. "He doesn't want to remind voters what a horrible mess the state is in."

"I-I-I don't get it," said Bennet. "If he's doing such a terrible job, wh-wh-why do people say they're going to vote for him again?"

"Because he keeps knocking the other candidate," said his father. "He keeps saying how bad the other guy is."

"Is he?" asked Bennet.

"He could be better," said Mr. Ordway. "But at least *he* talks about real issues."

"Dear," said Mrs. Ordway, looking at her husband. She touched her white napkin to her chin.

Mr. Ordway had a small splotch of red spaghetti sauce just below his lower lip. He wiped it off with his napkin. "Boy, would I love to write a series of articles exposing the governor for what he really is," said Mr. Ordway. Mr. Ordway was a reporter for the North Agaming *Sun,* the local newspaper, and covered the political scene in the state capital.

"Well, why don't you?" said Mrs. Ordway.

"Are you kidding? Stevenson would have my head," said Mr. Ordway. Mr. Stevenson was the publisher of *The Sun.* From what Bennet could make out, his father disagreed with nearly every decision Stevenson made in regard to the running of the newspaper. "Well, enough of this!" said Mr. Ordway. He picked up the remote control and began changing channels on the TV.

"Hey, D-d-dad," said Bennet. "I have something to show you."

"What's that?" asked Mr. Ordway, unable to decide whether to watch a game show or an old rerun of *I Love Lucy.* He kept switching back and forth between the two channels.

"This shortwave transmitter Pete and me—"

"Pete and *I*," corrected his mother, who was an English teacher at the local junior high school.

"Pete and I found," said Bennet.

"A transmitter?" said Mr. Ordway curiously, changing the channel again.

"Yeah. It's real old," said Bennet, who was a huge electronics buff. He and Pete Nickowsky, his best friend who lived next door, had discovered the shortwave transmitter that afternoon in the garbage Dumpster behind the local Grand Union. "Want to see it?"

"Sure," said his father.

"J-j-just lemme p-p-put it back together," said Bennet excitedly, leaping up from his chair.

"What about dessert?" asked Mrs. Ordway as she rose to clear the table.

Bennet didn't even bother to find out what dessert was. "I'll eat it later," he said, and raced downstairs to his father's toolroom in the cellar. There on the wooden workbench, among a jumble of wires, circuit panels, fuses, and old radio tubes, sat the ancient transmitter. It was a big, boxlike apparatus with a dull black finish and all sorts of interesting knobs and switches and a large numbered glass dial. Bennet and Pete had taken the whole thing apart to see how it was put together. It took Bennet less than forty minutes to reassemble the transmitter. Bennet stuck the knobs back on, then ran up the cellar stairs, calling, "Dad! Hey, Dad! W-w-wanna see it?"

He found his father in the living room. He was settled in front of the big TV, watching a basketball game. Mr. Ordway had his shoes off and his feet up on the mahogany coffee table.

The moment Bennet walked into the room, his father held up his hand, palm out, indicating that he should be quiet. A basketball player on TV was dribbling quickly down the court to the enthusiastic roar of the people in the stands.

"It's *show time!*" shouted the sportscaster fervently as the tall, skinny player leaped up and slammed the ball into the basketball hoop.

"Yesss!" exclaimed Mr. Ordway. He turned to Bennet and said, "I'll be right down. As soon as the next commercial comes on."

Bennet returned to the toolroom to wait. He waited for about twenty minutes, and then he went back upstairs. Mr. Ordway was still glued to the TV set. "It's almost over," he said. "Just let me see who wins. Why don't you sit down and watch?"

But Bennet had no interest in basketball. He was fascinated by things that ran on electricity, not by an electric moment in a basketball game—or any game, for that matter. Down in the toolroom,

Bennet waited for what seemed like ages, and then he marched back upstairs.

"D-d-dad! Hey, Dad!" he said. Entering the living room, he saw his father in his chair, head down, asleep, snoring.

"Don't wake your father, Bennet," said his mother as she came into the room with a stack of her students' tests to correct. She had changed into her slippers. "He's had a long day."

The Transmitter

Bennet and Pete hung out together every day after school. They had a routine. First they fed Pete's black Labrador retriever, Gus. Then they went over to Bennet's house and got themselves something to eat. They ate anything and everything—cookies, peanut butter-and-jelly sandwiches, popcorn, cereal, marshmallows, pickles. Seated at the kitchen table, they leafed through magazines while they ate. Because the Ordways subscribed to many magazines, Bennet and Pete had plenty to choose from.

After they finished eating, the two boys usually ventured down to the toolroom to work on their latest project. One day it was a solar-powered mousetrap; another day, a skateboard with headlights. Bennet liked being home on weekday afternoons. Since both his parents worked, the house was always nice and quiet, with no distractions. Nobody was around to tell him to take out the garbage or to be sure to rinse out his dirty glass and put it in the dishwasher.

That next afternoon was like any other week-day afternoon. Bennet and Pete came home from school, fed Gus, had a snack (pretzels and milk), and then headed down to the toolroom to tinker with the transmitter. Bennet drilled a hole in the back of the transmitter and hooked up a jack. Then he wired the transmitter's components to an old microwave oven that, much to Bennet's horror, his mother had actually intended to throw away. Using a pair of wire strippers, he spliced a wire here, snipped one there. Bennet had his very own tool chest. His pride and joy, the tool chest was crammed with all sorts of tools and screws and col-ored wires and electronic gizmos and gadgets that he had rescued from discarded appliances. Open-ing the lid to Bennet's toolbox was like opening a treasure chest of hardware store supplies—and, to Bennet, that's exactly what his toolbox was: a treasure.

Bennet and Pete made many adjustments to the transmitter—some minor, some major. When they had finished, they made a trip to B & G's Hard-ware. Although there were other hardware stores much closer than B & G's, none was nearly as good. The merchandise at B & G's wasn't just reasonable; it was downright cheap. The same seven-piece screwdriver set that sold for $7.99 at the hardware store in the Grand Union shopping center was only $2.49 at B & G's. Everything, from alkaline batteries to zigzag rules, was a bargain at B & G's. B & G's was in the rundown section of town where the old brick textile mills stood, abandoned, and where many of the storefronts were boarded up. The truth was, assuming you didn't live right nearby, you would never travel to shop at B & G's—unless, of course, you happened to be two boys who were great bargain hunters.

The moment Jimmy, the owner of B & G's, saw Bennet and Pete walk into the store, his face lit up. He was always delighted to see them. "Well, look who's here!" he said with a big smile.

"Hi, J-j-jimmy," said Bennet. Even though Jimmy was close to sixty years old and had gray hair, Bennet and Pete called him by his first name. He told them to. He insisted on it, in fact.

"What brings you fellas here today?" asked Jimmy.

"We had nothing better to do, so we thought we'd come by and bug you," said Pete, stepping over to the counter, where a pair of old red leather boxing gloves lay. They were Jimmy's. Years ago, he had been a boxer. On the wall above the cash register, there was a framed black-and-white photograph of Jimmy as a young man in his boxing gloves and gear. He stood with his knees bent and his dukes up, as though he were about to land a blow at the photographer.

Pete slipped on the gloves and danced about on the wooden floor, punching at an imaginary foe. "He jabs with his left, he hooks with his right," cried Pete in the raspy voice of a ringside announcer. "Can nothing stop the White Knight?"

Jimmy roared with laughter. He had a loud, wonderful laugh. "I'll tell you who can stop the White Knight," he said. "The Black Knight!" That's what Jimmy used to call himself as a boxer, the Black Knight.

"Y-y-you know, Jimmy," said Bennet as, smiling, he looked about, "this place needs a g-g-good painting. When's the last time it was painted?"

Pete took off the boxing gloves and stepped over to the paint section. The shelves were lined with cans of house paint. "Let's see," said Pete. He picked up a gallon can of paint. "I think a nice lavender would really perk this place up."

"How about hot p-p-pink?" asked Bennet.

"You paint this place hot pink and I'll paint your butt hot pink," said Jimmy.

"Actually," said Bennet. "We need an ant-t-tenna."

Jimmy led the way to the electrical section. Not that they needed to be led, of course. Both Bennet and Pete knew the store by heart.

"How much is this one?" asked Bennet, picking up a small indoor TV/FM antenna. The antenna, when pulled out, resembled a rabbit's ears.

"This one?" said Jimmy, taking out his bifocals from the pocket of his flannel shirt. He put on his glasses to examine the antenna. "This here antenna is six dollars."

Bennet counted his money. He was short one dollar.

"Tell you what," said Jimmy. "You owe me." As it was, the two boys already owed him close to thirty dollars. Whenever they didn't have quite enough money to pay in full, Jimmy just said, "You owe me."

Bennet smiled. "Y-y-you got a deal. Thanks."

As Bennet and Pete were leaving the hardware store, Jimmy called after them, "Don't forget to tell your friends about us." He always called that out as they were on their way out the door.

When they returned to the toolroom, Bennet placed the microwave oven on the transmitter.

Then he and Pete lifted the transmitter and lugged it upstairs to Bennet's bedroom on the second floor of the house. They gently set the transmitter down on a trunk by the dormer window. Bennet attached the antenna's wires to the transmitter. Then he had Pete run down to his garage and bring up his sledding saucer. Bennet rigged the antenna to the round aluminum sled. He opened the window and set the improvised dish antenna on the shingled roof that sloped underneath. Looking out his window, Bennet could see Mt. Coolidge in the distance. Mt. Coolidge was the highest point in the area; all the local radio and TV stations had their transmitters on top of the mountain.

"Okay," said Bennet as he pulled his head back into the room. "Let's see if this thing works." He picked up the video camera that lay on his bed. It was Pete's father's video camera, but he never used it. Pete's parents were divorced. When Pete's father moved out of the house, he left a lot of his personal things behind, including the video camera. He said he was going to come by and collect it one day, but he never had.

"What should I do?" asked Pete, which is what Pete always asked whenever they were about to conduct an experiment. Bennet was really the inventor. Pete's specialty was writing.

"Go over to your house and t-t-turn on the TV," said Bennet. "Let me know if anything happens."

"You got it, Alva," said Pete. Alva was the nickname Pete had coined for Bennet. He got the name from the great inventor, Thomas Edison, whose middle name was Alva. Pete thought Alva was the most hysterical name.

After Pete left the room, Bennet stood beside his window and looked out. Down below, he saw Pete leave the house, cross the narrow strip of lawn between their houses, and disappear into his own house. Bennet plugged a cord into the video camera. Bending down, he inserted the other end of the cord into the transmitter. He flicked on the power switch to the transmitter.

At first, nothing happened. Then there was a soft hum and the dial on the face of the transmitter glowed green. Bennet glanced about his cluttered room for something to film. He had plenty of subject matter to choose from: his glow-in-the-dark globe and Sony Walkman, which were on his desk; the "Don't Even Think of Parking Here" street sign, which was on the wall above his desk; the enormous map of the United States, which was on the wall above his brass bed; plus the other things that decorated his walls: a large periodic table of the elements; an American flag; a poster of every type of knot known to seaman; another poster that depicted numerous space missiles; and still another poster that showed every flag in the world; not to mention his two gerbils, which he kept in an aquarium on his bookcase.

But Bennet didn't film any of these things. Instead, he looked down at his feet. He kicked off his right sneaker, pulled off his sock. He stood in the middle of the room and focused the camera lens directly at his naked foot. He filmed his toes, wiggling. Then he zoomed in on his big toe.

Just then, the upstairs phone rang. Bennet turned off the transmitter, set the video camera on his desk, and walked down to his parents' bedroom. He picked up the phone, which sat on the little night table beside his parents' bed.

"It works!" cried Pete's excited voice on the other end.

"It does? Really?" said Bennet. "What d-d-did you see?"

"Your model battleship."

"I didn't film my battleship."

"I'm just kidding," said Pete. "I saw your toes. They were on TV. By the way, your toenails need clipping."

Bennet was absolutely thrilled that the experiment had worked. Hanging up the phone, he threw a fist into the air and shouted, "Yesss!"

• • •

That evening at dinner Mr. Ordway asked Bennet what he had done that afternoon.

"Not much," replied Bennet.

"Play any football?" asked his father.

Bennet shook his head. "No."

"Hoop?"

Again, Bennet shook his head and answered, "No."

"I don't know why I went to all the trouble to put up that basketball net over the garage," said Mr. Ordway. "You never use it." Then Mr. Ordway asked Bennet if he had watched any TV that afternoon.

"No," said Bennet.

"Why, what was on TV?" asked Mrs. Ordway.

"Well," said Mr. Ordway. "It's the weirdest thing. Channel Six received calls from people in our neighborhood. Apparently, someone's foot suddenly appeared on their TV screens while they were watching TV."

"You're k-k-kidding!" blurted Bennet. He was shocked to find out that the transmitter could broadcast onto other people's TV sets.

"Someone's *foot*?" said Bennet's mother, scrunching up her nose.

Mr. Ordway nodded and said, "There's going to be a little article about it in tomorrow's paper."

Bennet was about to tell his father who the foot belonged to, but, on second thought, he changed his mind. He was worried it might get him into trouble.

A Brilliant Idea

The next morning as they were on their way to school, Bennet informed Pete that he wasn't the only one who had seen his foot on TV yesterday. Other people in the neighborhood had seen it on their TV sets, too.

"You lie like a rug," said Pete.

"It's t-t-true," said Bennet. "It was on Channel Six."

"You're telling me the transmitter can broadcast farther than my house?"

"I-I-I was surprised, too," said Bennet. "We must've b-b-broadcast on Channel Six's frequency without realizing it. There's even going to be a newsp-p-paper article about it. I tried to call you last night, but your line was busy."

"Really? We're in the paper?" said Pete excitedly as they walked along the cement sidewalk, past a house with a large tree in the front lawn. The tree was ablaze with orange leaves. It was a chilly morning, though not chilly enough to see your breath. "That's great!"

"Well, we're not in the paper," said Bennet. "My f-f-foot is."

Pete laughed. Pete, who had long blond hair that he tucked behind his ears, was wearing his denim jacket. It was his trademark—that and his high green sneakers and the Frisbee he always carried around in his backpack. "We've got to pick up a paper," he told Bennet.

"We can get one at the newsp-p-paper vending machine near the school," said Bennet. Bennet's trademark was his Boston Red Sox baseball cap and his Swiss army knife. Bennet never went anywhere without his trusty Swiss army knife.

The vending machine was on the corner of Cherry and Lincoln Streets, near a mailbox. The newspaper displayed in the square window of the vending machine showed a photograph of the governor with a headline that read: GOVERNOR ATTACKS OPPONENT ON FAMILY VALUES. Pete took out four dimes from the outside pocket of his backpack and dropped the dimes, one by one, into the coin slot. He pulled open the vending machine and removed the top paper. With Bennet looking on, he searched the front page for the article. "I don't see it," said Pete.

"T-t-try the next page," said Bennet.

Pete turned to the next page. There was an article about a whale that had washed up on a Cape Cod beach and an article about a small oil spill in the Mediterranean, plus a large advertisement for a pre-Election Day sale that a local department store was having on all famous-maker-brand women's winter coats, but no mention whatsoever of Bennet's foot. It wasn't until Pete turned to page 26, way in the back of the paper by the classified ads, that Bennet spotted the article. It was a tiny article, no more than a few sentences long. It was what, in newspaper jargon, is referred to as a filler.

Pete was appalled. "Look how small it is!" he said.

"What does it say?" asked Bennet.

Pete read the article out loud.

Mystery Toes Appear on TV

by Tom Ordway

Staff Writer

Oct. 19—Was your TV signal suddenly interrupted by the appearance of wiggling toes yesterday afternoon? Residents of the West Hill section of town who had their sets tuned to Channel 6 complained of seeing a foot instead of their regularly scheduled program. "I was watching

Oprah Winfrey when this big, ugly foot came on my TV," said Betty Campbell of 28 Tucker Street. WECD, the local TV station that was affected by the mysterious transmission, was unable to offer an explanation for the toes' appearance.

Pete looked up from the paper. "That's all it says."

"I-I-I don't think my f-f-foot is so ugly," said Bennet.

"The biggest news story of the day and they bury it in the back of the paper," said Pete, looking thoroughly disgusted. "What a crummy newspaper!"

"Hey!" said Bennet, taking offense. "My d-d-dad wrote that article."

"We should've been on the front page instead of this bozo," said Pete, slapping the back of his hand across the photograph of the governor.

"Well, if it makes you feel any b-better, my dad would probably agree," said Bennet.

"So why do they put him on the front page all the time?"

"Dad says it's because of Stevenson."

"Who's Stevenson?" asked Pete as they walked.

"The p-p-publisher of the paper," said Bennet. "He's a g-good friend of the governor. They go fishing together."

"Figures it'd be something like that," said Pete.

Bennet pointed to the governor's photograph. "See all those p-p-people waving American flags," he said. "My dad says it's all show. The governor has p-p-people who hand the flags out."

Pete stared at Bennet in disbelief. "Are you kidding me?"

Bennet shook his head.

"So when we see the governor on TV, we think everyone's in love with him," said Pete.

"You got it," said Bennet. "He also makes sure he only appears in very p-p-picturesque places."

"I guess that means he won't be visiting Broad Street anytime soon," said Pete. Broad Street was where B & G's Hardware was located.

"I guess not," said Bennet. "D-d-dad says he's going to be in this area tomorrow night. He's giving a big speech on TV. He's even b-b-busing in his supporters so he'll be seen in front of a big crowd."

"No!"

"Yes!"

"That's terrible!"

"That's slimy!" said Bennet. Sometimes Bennet and Pete got into a battle of words—a kind of verbal tug-of-war—to see who could top the other.

"That's despicable!"

"That's out-r-r-ragous!"

Stepping off the sidewalk, they cut across the school football field. The grass was wet with dew; their sneakers got soaked. Just beyond the football field was the soccer field, and just beyond the soccer field was the school. The school consisted of a series of single-level, flat-roofed brick buildings. "Say, Alva," said Pete as they passed under the football goalpost. "What would we need to do to make the transmitter broadcast a farther distance?"

"How much farther?"

"Oh, I don't know. A hundred miles or so."

"A hundred miles!" exclaimed Bennet. "Even Channel Six can't broadcast that far."

"How far can they broadcast?" asked Pete.

Bennet shrugged. "I don't know. Maybe forty or f-f-fifty miles."

"Well, then," said Pete. "What would we need to do to broadcast forty or fifty miles?"

"You're t-t-talking a television transmitter one hundred times more powerful than ours!"

"I am?" said Pete.

"The only way we could broadcast that far is if we were able to override Channel Six's t-t-transmitter on top of Mt. Coolidge. There's no way our little transmitter could do that."

"Oh, well," said Pete. "It was just a thought."

"I wonder, though . . ." said Bennet, still thinking about it.

Pete glanced at Bennet, who had a distant look in his eye. It was a look Pete had seen many times before. Bennet loved challenges. The bigger the challenge, the better. "You wonder what?" asked Pete.

"I wonder if we could interrupt Channel Six's studio-to-transmitter link."

"Channel Six's *what*?" said Pete.

"Studio-to-t-t-transmitter link," said Bennet. "It would be a much weaker signal."

"What's a studio-to-transmitter link?"

"That's the signal Channel Six's studio sends to its main transmitter up on Mt. Coolidge. You've seen that small d-d-dish antenna that's on the roof of the Holiday Inn in town, haven't you?"

"Sure," said Pete. "What about it?"

"That small antenna is Channel Six's studio transmitter," explained Bennet. "It transmits a signal up to their main transmitter on Mt. Coolidge. If I'm right about this, it'd only t-t-take about six gigahertz to interrupt it."

"That's *all*?" said Pete, trying to sound as if he knew what a gigahertz was.

"And if that's the case," continued Bennet, "it's very possible we could override that signal and b-b-broadcast our own signal."

"We could?" said Pete.

"We could," replied Bennet. "We'd need a bigger ant-t-tenna, though. It'd have to be up a lot higher, too. We'd also need to make the transmitter more powerful." He turned and looked inquisitively at Pete. "Why, what d-d-do you have in mind?"

Pete broke into a fiendish grin. "Well," he said, "what if, as the governor is making his speech on TV tomorrow, a really weird thing happens?"

"Like what?"

"Oh, I don't know," said Pete. "What if everyone's TV signal is mysteriously interrupted?"

Bennet stared at Pete. "You're not th-thinking what I think you're thinking."

Pete nodded.

Bennet laughed. "You're crazy!"

"It's a brilliant idea, you do have to admit," said Pete.

"Oh, it's in-ge-ge-genious!" said Bennet.

"Dastardly!" said Pete, rubbing his hands together.

"Insane!" said Bennet.

"What are we waiting for?" asked Pete as, off in the distance, the late bell rang.

"School!" said Bennet.

The Old Mead Place

On a small side street just off Broad Street stood a large Victorian house that had been abandoned for years. Tall weeds grew in the front yard, and the white paint on the house had faded to a dull gray. The windows on the second and third floors were smashed, and the magnificent bay window on the first floor was boarded up. If this house had stood anywhere else in town, people would still be living in it and taking care of it. The house would still be brightly painted; the lawn still mowed; and the flower beds still blooming with marigolds, chrysanthemums, dahlias, roses, and snapdragons. The house, in short, would still be loved. But the house was in the rundown section of town and, as a result, it was now empty, in a terrible state of disrepair.

Most everything in the old Mead place had long ago disappeared. Over the years people had broken into the house and taken anything that looked the least bit desirable—the brass door knocker, light fixtures, stained-glass windows, even the glass doorknobs from the closet doors. The fact was, not counting the house itself, there was only one thing of any value that still remained on the property, although few knew it existed and even fewer considered it valuable. And that was the large VHF/UHF TV antenna that was perched on top of the roof.

. . .

Bennet knew about the antenna. He had seen it many times on his way to B & G's Hardware. He knew there must be *something* he and Pete could use the old antenna for, but he had never been able to think of anything—until now.

"So how are we g-g-going to do this?" asked Bennet as he and Pete made their way through the high grass and weeds in the front yard. It was late afternoon, and the light was fading. They had intentionally come at this hour so it would be difficult for anyone to spot them in the murky light.

"Well," said Pete, "we can probably get on the roof from one of the third-floor windows."

"No, I mean when we b-b-broadcast during the governor's speech," said Bennet, who had brought along his backpack. The backpack, which was filled with tools, weighed a ton. It also rattled. "We're not going to show my f-f-foot again, are we?"

"No," said Pete, shaking his head. "We'll have to think of something else."

"Hey, I have a thought," said Bennet. "We could wear masks and g-g-go on the air."

"Oh, sure, that'll fool everyone," said Pete. He stopped in front of an old, rusty drainpipe that ran up the rear of the house to the second floor. He reached into his back pocket and pulled out a pair of black leather winter gloves. "A masked boy with a stutter. Nobody will know who *that* is."

Bennet had to admit that Pete had a point. "Who's going up first?" he asked.

"I'll go," said Pete, slipping on his gloves.

Pete grabbed hold of the drainpipe and shimmied up to a slender window on the second floor. He squeezed through the narrow window. Once Pete was in the house, Bennet put on his cotton work gloves and climbed up the drainpipe.

"I'll tell you one thing," said Pete, giving Bennet a hand as he crawled through the window. "If I go on TV, my mom will know it's me. I guarantee it. She has this sixth sense."

"Even with a m-m-mask?" asked Bennet, stepping on some broken glass and bathroom tiles.

They had come in through the upstairs bathroom. It was dark inside the house. Bennet unzipped his backpack, took out two flashlights, and handed one to Pete.

"Even with a mask," said Pete, clicking on his flashlight.

The two boys walked up a narrow staircase that led to the third floor. They entered a tiny room that, years ago, had once been a servant's bed-room.

"It's k-k-kind of creepy being here at this time of d-day," said Bennet. He yanked open the tiny window. Stooping, he crawled out the window, onto the roof.

"You're telling me," said Pete as he, too, crawled outside.

The boys inched across the roof to the chimney, where the antenna was. The antenna was attached to the bricks on the chimney by a bracket and bolts. Bennet and Pete squatted beside the chimney and inspected the bolts.

"They look pretty rusty," said Pete, shining his flashlight beam on the corroded bolts that were screwed into the chimney bricks.

But Bennet had come prepared. "Nothing a lit-tle rust d-d-dissolvent can't take care of," he said. He reached into his backpack and pulled out a can of Liquid Wrench. Aiming the nozzle at the rusty bolts, he sprayed. Then he took out his Swiss army knife and, opening the screwdriver section, went to work.

"Hold the ant-t-tenna, will ya," Bennet instructed Pete as he unloosened one of the bolts. "I don't want this thing f-f-falling on me."

Pete clutched the antenna. With each bolt Bennet removed, the antenna became wobblier and wobblier. "Hold it tight," said Bennet, glancing up at Pete. Pete was staring at something over across the street. "What are you looking at?"

"That dog," said Pete, with a nod of his head.

Bennet looked over and saw a stray white dog across the street. The dog was sniffing some bushes in front of a house.

"I just had a brainstorm," said Pete. "I know who could go on the air for us."

"Who?"

"Gus."

"Gus?" said Bennet. "You mean, G-g-gus your dog?"

"Yeah," said Pete. "There are so many black Labs, nobody will know whose dog it is. Or better yet, we'll put a mask on him!" He was getting very excited. "I could stand off-camera and talk for him."

"I have an even b-b-better idea," said Bennet. "What if we use my two gerbils?"

Pete scoffed. "Your *ger*bils?"

"Yeah," said Bennet. "They could rate the g-g-governor's performance. You know, like those two movie critics on TV."

"Gus is a lot more photogenic than your gerbils," said Pete. Clearly, he was offended that Bennet hadn't liked his idea of using Gus.

"B-b-but everyone loves gerbils," insisted Bennet.

"Not as much as they love dogs," said Pete.

"But gerbils are cute."

"Can your gerbils roll over?" demanded Pete. "Can they sit up and beg? Or catch a Frisbee?"

"Well, no."

"Gus can!"

Bennet didn't want to get into a big argument. "All right. All right," he said. "W-w-we'll use Gus."

But Pete was not to be mollified. He could get pretty touchy sometimes—particularly about his dog. He loved Gus. He had taught the dog all kinds of tricks. "I can't believe you think your gerbils are cuter than Gus. They can't hold a candle to Gus."

Bennet removed a rope from his backpack. He

tied one end to the antenna. Holding the other end of the rope tightly, Bennet and Pete carefully lowered the antenna down to the back lawn. The moment it touched the ground, Pete said, "I don't know about you, but I'm out of here. It's spooky being in this house after dark."

"Wh-wh-what was that?" asked Bennet as he followed Pete through the third-floor window.

Pete froze. He beamed his flashlight onto Bennet's face. "What was what?"

"That noise."

"What noise?"

"Y-y-you didn't hear it?"

"No," said Pete. "And what's more, I'm not sticking around to hear it." He fled down the stairs.

"Hey, wait for me!" cried Bennet. Shining his flashlight in front of him, he ran down the stairs. When he reached the bottom of the stairs, something leaped out at him from the darkened hallway.

"Boooo!" shouted Pete.

Bennet nearly had a heart attack. "You jerk!" he said. And then he broke into laughter.

Dress Rehearsal

The next day after school Bennet and Pete made another trip to B & G's Hardware, this time to purchase more powerful radio tubes— the most powerful and, as it turned out, the only radio tubes B & G's carried. Transistors long ago replaced vacuum tubes in things like shortwaves, radios, and television sets.

"What are you fellas building, anyway?" asked Jimmy as he carried an old cardboard box of radio tubes up from the cellar. "An antique radio?"

"No, b-b-but that's not a bad idea," said Bennet. He was deliberately being vague. He didn't want anybody—not even his friend Jimmy—to know what he and Pete were up to.

Jimmy set the box on the counter. "Will these do?" he asked.

The box held nine gigantic radio tubes. Pete pulled one out. The domed top was caked with dust. The radio tubes must have been over fifty years old.

Pete inspected the radio tube and then showed it to Bennet. Bennet examined it closely to make sure the tubes would fit in the transmitter and then nodded.

Turning to Jimmy, Pete said, "We'll take 'em."

"They don't make these anymore," said Jimmy. "So I hope that's all you need."

"How m-m-much do they cost?" asked Bennet. He was worried that, being so rare, the radio tubes were going to cost a fortune.

"This box has been down in the cellar since I bought the place, and not one person has ever asked for one," said Jimmy. "Tell you what. I'll give you the whole batch for a penny."

Bennet smiled. "You drive a hard bargain, Jimmy."

The first thing Bennet and Pete did when they got back to Bennet's bedroom was to add the more powerful radio tubes to the transmitter. Then they hooked up an antenna wire to the back of the transmitter. They ran the wire out of Bennet's window and across the roof and over to a tall maple tree that grew beside the house. Using a staple gun, Bennet stapled the wire under the shingle flaps so it was all but invisible. Then he attached the wire to the huge antenna that they had taken from the old Mead place. He had already hooked up his sledding saucer to the antenna. The antenna and aluminum disk were way up high in the tree, hidden among brightly colored fall leaves.

"Time for a dress rehearsal," said Pete once they had finished. "I'll get Gus." He hurried over to his house. He returned a few moments later with Gus tied to a red leash.

Upon entering Bennet's bedroom, Gus went berserk. First, he insisted on sniffing the wastepaper basket under Bennet's desk. Then he sniffed Bennet's sneakers, which were under the bed. Then he sniffed a white sock that lay on the floor in Bennet's closet.

"He's k-k-kind of excited, isn't he?" asked Bennet. He picked up his lamp, which was on the small table beside his bed, so Gus wouldn't knock it over with his tail. Gus's tail was wagging back and forth.

"He's just never seen your room before," said Pete. "Gus, no!" he cried. Yanking the leash, Pete pulled Gus away. The dog had started to climb up onto Bennet's bed.

"Y-y-you don't think he's t-too excited, do you?"

"He'll calm down in a minute," said Pete. "Gus, stop it!" He gave the leash another yank. Gus had put his front paws up on Bennet's desk.

"He has to be still in front of the camera, you know."

"I know," said Pete.

"Otherwise he'll j-j-just be a blur. A b-big blur."

"I understand," said Pete as Gus pulled him over to Bennet's bookcase.

"Gerbils never get excited," said Bennet.

"Gus, no!" shouted Pete. Gus had discovered the gerbil aquarium in Bennet's bookcase. He pressed his nose to the aquarium glass, fogging it up. "Calm down!" Pete ordered the dog. He pushed Gus's rump down to the carpeted floor. "Sit!" he commanded sternly. Gus, panting heavily, sat. "There! That's better," said Pete, patting the dog on his head. He reached into his pants pocket, pulled out a dog biscuit, and gave it to Gus. "Now behave yourself," he said. Gus ate the dog biscuit in one bite.

"Well, let's try a practice run," said Bennet. He picked up the video camera from his desk and put it to his eye. He peered at Gus. "G-g-gus, I'm over here."

"Look this way, Gus," instructed Pete, pointing toward Bennet.

Tongue hanging out, Gus looked over at Bennet.

"G-g-good boy!" said Bennet as he focused the camera lens.

"Hey, want Gus to do his dog-biscuit trick on TV?" asked Pete. He was referring to the trick in which Gus balanced a dog biscuit on the tip of his nose and, at Pete's command, tossed the biscuit up into the air and caught it in his mouth. Pete was extremely proud of the trick.

"Let's save it f-f-for later," said Bennet. "Right now, I think we should have you p-p-practice speaking to the camera."

"Okey-doke," said Pete. Disguising his voice, Pete began to speak in a highly animated, cartoon-like voice. He sounded like Goofy, the Walt Disney dog. "I think this governor's race is going to the dogs!" he said. He let out a loud, goofy laugh.

"Cut!" said Bennet, like a big Hollywood director. He put the camera down. "This isn't g-g-going to work."

"What isn't?" said Pete, a trifle annoyed.

"This. Y-y-you can't just talk off the t-t-top of your head."

"Why not?"

"B-b-because," said Bennet, "y-y-you're going to be talking to a lot of people. It has to be thought out in advance. C-c-carefully thought out."

"But I liked what I said about the governor's race going to the dogs," protested Pete.

"You can still say that," said Bennet. "I-I-I just meant we should think about what you're going to say. W-w-we need to write it out."

"You're right," said Pete. "I don't know why I didn't think of that myself." He sat down at Bennet's desk and sharpened a pencil in the electric pencil sharpener. "I've never written a speech before, but this seems like the perfect time to start."

Pete and Bennet spent the next hour working on the speech. They had no trouble finding subjects to talk about. Bennet just remembered the things he had heard his father say about the governor. In fact, in places, Pete wrote down Bennet's exact words—which were really Mr. Ordway's exact words. At first, the two boys tried to touch on everything—unemployment, crime, drugs, school funding, the state deficit—but when Pete read the speech out loud, it sounded too long and muddled. So Pete rewrote the speech, keeping it short and sweet—or, depending on how you looked at it, short and nasty.

"Now what are we going to do about a mask?" asked Pete.

Bennet went to his closet. He removed two

masks from a hook on the other side of his closet door. He had worn one of the masks last Halloween; the other mask he had found in a trash can in front of a neighbor's house. "You have a choice." He held up the masks for Pete to see. "Dracula or F-f-frankenstein."

Pete took the masks. He squatted in front of Gus and said, "Since you have such fanglike teeth, Gus, I think you should be Dracula." He tried to slip the mask on Gus, but the dog wouldn't let him. He pulled it off with his paw.

"Tell you what," said Pete. "So you don't feel alone, I'll wear a mask, too." He pulled the Frankenstein mask over his face. Then he put the Dracula mask on Gus. This time the mask stayed on.

"Good boy!" exclaimed Pete. To show Gus how pleased he was, Pete rubbed him under his chin and gave him another dog biscuit.

The Governor's Speech

At exactly eight o'clock that evening, Bennet poked his head into his mother's study. "Aren't you g-g-going to watch the g-g-governor's speech?" he asked.

His mother looked up from her desk, where she was reading some student reports. A desk lamp shone on her brown hair. "What for?" she asked. "I already know what he's going to say. Nothing."

Bennet walked into the living room. The house was unusually quiet because his father, who normally would have been home watching TV, was working late that night. He was covering the governor's speech for the paper. Bennet turned on the TV and put on Channel 6. A news commentator appeared on the screen and said that the governor would be beginning his speech momentarily. The screen switched to a podium, and a man's voice announced, "Ladies and gentlemen, the governor." The governor strode across the stage to wild applause from the people in the auditorium. Nearly everyone in the audience was holding a small American flag, which they swirled about in the air. Beaming, the governor stood at the podium and waved to the crowd. He waited until the applause died down, and then he looked right into the camera and said in a very solemn voice, "I'd like to talk to you tonight about something that's destroying the very moral fabric of this great state. Indeed, of this great country. And that's the state of our family." The governor removed his glasses and continued, "Things have gotten way out of hand. Now my challenger would have you believe—"

Bennet never heard what the governor thought his challenger would have him believe because he clicked off the TV set. He walked out of the room and up the stairs. His bedroom door was closed. Bennet's heart pounded as he reached for the doorknob.

Pete and Gus were seated on his bedroom floor, in front of his bed. Pete did not look up when Bennet entered the room; he was rehearsing his speech. He had the speech printed on small white index cards. Again and again, Pete mumbled to himself the opening lines. To disguise his voice, he held a folded bandanna over his mouth. The bandanna muffled his voice.

Bennet walked to his desk and picked up the

video camera. He lifted the camera to his eye. His hands trembled. He placed his finger on the button that, when pushed, would begin the filming, and peered through the lens at Pete. Pete looked pale and nervous. He picked up a glass of water that was sitting on the floor, but his hand shook so violently that he put the glass down. Pete lowered the Dracula mask over Gus's face and slipped the Frankenstein mask over his own face. He raised the bandanna to his mouth. Bennet focused tightly in on Gus's Dracula mask and began to film.

"We interrupt this speech to bring you the following unpaid political commentary," boomed Pete off-camera, holding the bandanna to his mouth, talking like a TV announcer. Then he changed his voice to sound like a cartoon character. "Hey, Governor, how come you never talk about real issues like unemployment? Cat got your tongue? You tell me what cat it is, and I'll chase after it. All you ever seem to talk about, Governor, is family values. But even then you don't talk about real family values. I'm talking about families that make their dogs sit up and beg for their dinner. What kind of values are those? And families that make their dogs roll over. How humiliating can you get! The dog gets all dirty just for some family's amusement. So, Governor, if you're going to talk about family values, talk about *real* family values! I tell you, the governor's race is going to the dogs! The dogs!"

Bennet continued to film Gus for a couple of more moments, and then he stopped the camera and put it down. "N-n-n-now l-l-let's see wh-what happens," he said, stuttering more than usual.

• • •

They didn't have to wait long. Within minutes, the phone rang. Bennet didn't dare answer it. He crept down to the foot of the stairs to listen in on his mother's conversation.

"You're kidding!" he heard his mother say from her study. "A dog wearing a Dracula mask? I'm sorry I missed it. Nobody has a clue?" A long pause followed, and then his mother said, "Oh, sure. How late do you think you'll be? I'll wait up for you." Bennet heard his mother hang up the phone. Turning, he hurried back up the stairs.

"Who was it?" Pete asked when Bennet entered the bedroom.

"M-m-my dad," said Bennet. "He c-called to tell my m-m-mom about Gus and that he's g-g-got to work late."

"Well, we're out of here," said Pete. He grabbed Gus by the collar. Pete and Gus waited at the top of the stairs while Bennet crept down to the front hallway to make sure his mother wasn't around. His mother had left her study and was now in the living room. Bennet could hear her zapping the TV channels. Keeping his eye on the living room doorway, Bennet signaled Pete; Pete grabbed Gus by the collar and rushed down the stairs. Bennet hurried over and opened the front door for them. Pete was about to step outside when a police car, which happened to be cruising the neighborhood, drove slowly by the house. Pete leaped back inside, yanking Gus in with him.

"Whew!" he said after the police car had disappeared down the block. "I guess I'm more nervous than I realize. Well, see you tomorrow."

Bennet closed the door. He was about to return upstairs to his bedroom when he changed his mind and headed for the living room.

"You'll never guess what happened," his mother said when he walked in. She was sitting less than two feet away from the TV set. If Bennet had been sitting that close to the TV, his mother would have told him to move back.

"What?" asked Bennet, taking a seat on the edge of the couch.

"The governor was giving his speech when apparently the TV signal was interrupted and a dog wearing a Dracula mask came on. Here, watch: They're going to show it again."

Bennet lifted his eyes to the TV. Gus appeared on the screen while, offscreen, Pete ranted and raved about the governor. Bennet had been so nervous while he was filming, he had been unable to hold the camera steady. The way the camera jerked about, you would have thought Bennet had just stepped off a roller coaster. His mother clapped her hands loudly with each point that was made. "This is great!" she exclaimed. "At least someone has the guts to tell it like it is—even if the person does hide behind a masked dog."

Bennet felt none of his mother's joy. He was still jittery from the broadcast. What's more, he was bothered by something he hadn't noticed while he was filming: Gus's mask was a little cockeyed. Fortunately, it wasn't enough to give Gus away. Still, it was something to worry about.

Deep Throat

Mr. Ordway didn't come home until a quarter to twelve that night. Although Bennet had gone to bed hours earlier, he was still wide awake in his darkened bedroom. He was too keyed up to sleep. Besides, he wanted to hear what his father had to say about the broadcast. Being a newspaper reporter, Mr. Ordway got the inside scoop on the news. When Bennet heard his father's voice in the kitchen, he climbed out of bed and came downstairs.

"Bennet!" said his mother, surprised, when he entered the kitchen. She was sitting at the kitchen table in her blue terrycloth bathrobe. "What are you doing up?"

"I-I-I couldn't sleep," said Bennet. He looked over at his father, who was leaning against the kitchen counter. He still had on his coat and tie. "Hi, Dad."

"Hey, Benny," said his father. He was in a good

mood. His father never called him Benny unless he was in a good mood.

"So, anyway," said Mr. Ordway, continuing the conversation he had begun with Mrs. Ordway, "the phones rang off the hook. We got calls from as far away as a radio station in Kansas wanting to know what was up."

"Wh-wh-what are you talking about?" asked Bennet, pretending he didn't know.

"A pirate broadcast interrupted the governor's televised speech tonight," said Mr. Ordway.

"Oh, yeah, M-m-mom and I saw it," said Bennet. "D-d-does anybody know who did it?"

Mr. Ordway shook his head. "Nobody has a clue. No person or group has claimed responsibility."

"What did the governor say about the dog?" asked Mrs. Ordway.

"He said it was just one more example of how we need tougher laws against criminals."

Mrs. Ordway made a face to indicate she didn't think much of the governor's response. "Typical," she said.

"Isn't it?" said Mr. Ordway. "If he was really serious about getting tough with criminals, he'd get tough on guns. But to get tough on guns would mean getting tough with the gun lobby."

"So what happened after the governor gave his speech?" asked Mrs. Ordway.

Mr. Ordway chuckled. "Everyone just questioned him about the dog. Nobody paid any attention to what the governor said in his speech."

Mrs. Ordway laughed.

"Boy, would I love to know more about this dog," said Mr. Ordway. "I mean, whoever did the broadcast. Someone said it may be an attention-getting stunt by the other candidate or just a practical joke, but I don't think so. I think it's someone who's sick and tired of the way things are." Mr. Ordway opened a cupboard and got himself a glass. He filled it with water from the faucet and took a sip. "Who knows, maybe the person or group behind this dog will bring down the governor. You know, like Deep Throat."

"What's D-d-deep Throat?" asked Bennet.

"You mean, *who* was Deep Throat," corrected his mother.

"Deep Throat was an anonymous source who helped reveal the Watergate break-in," said his father.

"What's W-w-watergate?" asked Bennet.

"The Watergate break-in took place back in nineteen seventy-two," said Mr. Ordway. "Five burglars were caught breaking into the Democratic

Party headquarters, which was located in the Watergate Hotel."

"These weren't just any old burglars, though," said Mrs. Ordway.

"No way," said Mr. Ordway. "These burglars were hired by the White House."

"The *White House*?" exclaimed Bennet. "Wh-wh-why were they breaking in?"

"To put in wiretap bugs so they could eavesdrop on the Democrats," said his father.

"Isn't that illegal?" asked Bennet, who knew all about wiretap bugs.

"Sure it is," said his father.

"Wh-wh-why did they do it then?" asked Bennet.

"To find out what the Democrats knew," said his father. "See, this happened back when Richard Nixon was president. He was running for reelection, and the Nixon people wanted to get information that they could use against the Democrats during the election."

"That's p-p-pretty slimy," said Bennet.

"Yes, it was," agreed Mr. Ordway. "Anyway, after the burglars were arrested, there was a big cover-up of who knew what about the break-in. Even the president was involved in the cover-up."

"How d-d-did they find this out?" asked Bennet.

"Two investigative reporters from *The Washington Post* uncovered the story."

"Wh-wh-what were the reporters' names?" asked Bennet.

"Bob Woodward and Carl Bernstein," replied Mr. Ordway quickly. He answered the question faster than he probably could have told you who the father of the country was. "Their reporting helped lead to a congressional hearing that eventually led President Nixon to resign."

"Wow!" said Bennet.

"The reporters did it through hard work, persistence, and Deep Throat," said Mr. Ordway admiringly.

"So who was D-d-deep Throat?" asked Bennet.

"Nobody knows," said Mr. Ordway.

"Except Woodward and Bernstein," said Mrs. Ordway.

"And Ben Bradlee—the editor of *The Washington Post* at the time," said Mr. Ordway. "Bob Woodward would meet with Deep Throat in a parking garage, and Deep Throat would give him clues about who was involved in the Watergate cover-up."

"It sounds f-f-fascinating," said Bennet.

"It was," said Mr. Ordway. "Those two guys—Woodward and Bernstein—were my heroes. Still are. In fact, it was because of them, really, that I became a reporter."

Mrs. Ordway abruptly stood up. "Will you look at what time it is!" she cried, glancing over at the clock on the wall. It was ten after twelve. "Time for this young man to hit the sack. Time for us all to hit the sack."

Bennet kissed his father good night and, though he had already kissed his mother good night earlier, he kissed her again, too, and then he went upstairs to his bedroom.

Late as it was, Bennet was unable to fall asleep. His mind was racing a hundred thoughts a second as he lay in bed staring up at his dark ceiling. He thought about the broadcast; the governor's response; the Watergate break-in; and those two reporters, Woodward and Bernstein. He also thought about his father and how excited he was tonight. Bennet had never seen him so happy. He loved hearing his father talk about the Watergate break-in and what happened afterward. His father hardly ever told him things like that. And to think it never would have happened if he and Pete hadn't made the broadcast.

Bennet rolled over onto his side. He gazed out his window at the dark, rolling outline of distant Mt. Coolidge. The red light on top of Channel 6's tall antenna was lit—as it always was at night—warning airplanes that there was an antenna on top of the mountain. Against the night sky, the red light blinked on and off, on and off, like a throbbing heart.

· · ·

Mr. Ordway was up extra early the next morning. He was anxious to get to the office, to see if there had been any new developments on the story about the dog that had interrupted the governor's speech. He was in such a rush to get to work, he didn't even sit down and have breakfast with the rest of his family. "I'll pick something up from Dunkin' Donuts," he told his wife as he left the house.

It had been very cold the night before, and the windows on his car were white with frost. Mr. Ordway hopped into the car and, pumping his foot on the gas pedal, turned the key in the ignition.

While the car warmed up, Mr. Ordway scraped the frost off the front windshield with a little scraper that he had received free from his insurance company. He was scraping the part of the windshield that was in front of the steering wheel when he noticed a small, folded piece of notebook paper under the windshield wiper. The lined paper felt cold, which meant it had been there for quite some time. Mr. Ordway unfolded the paper.

There was a message written in blue pen. It said:

STAY TUNED!

It was signed,

DEEP DOO-DOO

The Governor's Big Mistake

"**D**eep Doo-doo? Deep Doo-doo? What do you mean 'Deep Doo-doo'?" cried Pete later that morning after Bennet told him about the note he had left on his father's windshield.

"Shh," said Bennet, glancing nervously about. They were on their way to school. "Not so loud."

"Why did you sign it 'Deep Doo-doo'?" Pete demanded, trying to keep his voice down.

"B-b-because," said Bennet. "It's like D-d-deep Throat."

Pete made a face. "*Deep Throat?* What the heck is Deep Throat?"

"I-i-it's not what, it's who," said Bennet. "D-d-d-deep Throat was B-b-bob Woodward and Carl Bernstein's anon-n-nymous source."

"I'm supposed to know who they are?" said Pete.

"Woodward and B-b-bernstein were the two *Washington P-p-post* reporters who uncovered the Watergate break-in," explained Bennet. He then told Pete about the Watergate break-in and Deep Throat.

"All right," Pete said, "I understand everything but one thing. Why on earth did you sign it Deep Doo-doo? I mean, why didn't you sign it Deep Trouble or Deep Pockets or something?"

"B-b-because," said Bennet. "I-I-I didn't think of it."

"Deep Doo-doo," said Pete, shaking his head in disgust. "What kind of a name is that?" He looked at Bennet. "So what exactly did your note say?"

"Stay t-t-tuned," replied Bennet.

"That's it?" asked Pete.

"That's it," said Bennet.

"It's not much of a note."

Bennet just shrugged.

"Stay tuned sounds like there's more to come," said Pete.

"There is," said Bennet.

"There *is*?" echoed Pete, surprised. "What do you mean there is?"

"There's going to be another b-b-broadcast," said Bennet.

"Says *who*?"

"We have to make another b-b-broadcast," said Bennet. "There's still more to say."

"Nobody asked me if there should be another broadcast," said Pete.

"I would've," said Bennet, "but the idea c-c-came to me in the middle of the night."

"Correct me if I'm wrong," said Pete. "But it was *my* idea to broadcast during the governor's speech."

"I never said it wasn't," said Bennet.

"If you had thought up the idea, I would've consulted you before I decided there was going to be another broadcast. What's more, I never would have left a note referring to us as Deep Doo-doo."

"Look, I'm sorry," said Bennet. "I d-d-didn't think you'd mind."

But Pete did mind. Now his feelings were hurt. Pete said nothing more, and Bennet decided not to press it.

As they approached the corner of Cherry and Lincoln, where the newspaper vending machine was, Pete broke his silence, announcing: "We better not be on page twenty-six again; that's all I can say."

They weren't. They had made the front page. The headline was visible through the window on the vending machine: MYSTERY DOG INTERRUPTS GOVERNOR'S SPEECH! The article was written by Bennet's father. Not only that, but there was a big photograph on the front page of Gus in his Dracula mask.

"Now *that's* more like it!" exclaimed Pete as he quickly inserted nickels and dimes into the coin slot. He yanked open the vending machine door and reached in and pulled out a newspaper.

Pete read the story out loud to Bennet. When he had finished, he handed the paper to Bennet, saying, "One of your father's better-written articles, I think."

Bennet turned to the middle of the paper, where there were more articles on Gus. He read Pete the headlines on the other related articles. " 'Thousands Watch Mystery Dog on TV,' " he said. " 'Network T-t-technicians at WECD-TV Puzzled.' 'Woman Questioned by Police.' "

"Why did they question a woman?" asked Pete.

Bennet skimmed the article. "They think your voice sounded like a woman's."

"A *woman's!*" cried Pete, appalled. "My voice doesn't sound anything at all like a woman's!"

"She's a disgruntled f-f-former employee of Channel Six," said Bennet. "But she's not considered a suspect."

"I can't believe they think I sound like a woman," wailed Pete.

Bennet read the headline on the last article. " 'G-g-governor Calls Act Cowardly.' "

"*What!*" exclaimed Pete incredulously. He

snatched the paper out of Bennet's hands and began to read aloud. "In what he referred to as one of the most cowardly acts he has ever witnessed, the governor demanded that the person or persons responsible for last night's interruption of his speech come forward."

Pete, his eyes blazing mad, looked at Bennet. "Can you believe this guy?" he said. "That was one of the bravest things I've ever done, and he calls it cowardly! The nerve!" He handed the paper back to Bennet. "Ooooh, boy, does that burn me up!"

"L-l-listen to what else he says," said Bennet. He proceeded to read more of the article. " 'It's just another sad c-c-c-commentary on our m-m-morally bankrupt times.' "

"Now I'm mad," said Pete. "I'm not just mad: I'm really mad. No, I mean really, really mad. The governor has made a big mistake."

"A gi-gi-gigantic mistake," said Bennet.

"A colossal mistake," said Pete.

"A hu-m-m-mongous mistake," said Bennet.

Pete looked fiercely at Bennet and said, "Stay tuned, governor! Deep Doo-doo is broadcasting again!"

The Anonymous Source

Everywhere Bennet and Pete went that morning they heard about the mystery dog that had interrupted the governor's speech. The kids were buzzing about it on the school playground. The teachers mentioned it in class. Even the cafeteria workers and custodians could be heard asking one another if they had seen the dog with the Dracula mask on TV the night before.

Pete loved all the attention. Whenever he overheard someone in the hallway or on the playground talking about the broadcast, Pete would inch closer so he could hear better. Sometimes he joined in the conversation. If Bennet was around, he would wave to him to come over and join the conversation. But Bennet just shook his head and walked away. He was much too nervous to do anything like that. During social studies, the only class the boys shared, Pete passed Bennet a total of nine notes on topics they could address on their next broadcast. The topics ranged from the plight of the rain forests to how it should be illegal for companies to call you up during dinnertime and try and sell you their merchandise. Bennet was terrified that old Ms. Brinkley, their teacher, would notice Pete slipping notes to him, but luckily she didn't. She was too involved in leading a discussion on who might have been responsible for last night's strange broadcast. She was convinced it was some fringe group with a secret agenda.

School let out at 2:30. Bennet and Pete were back at Bennet's house by 2:41—a record. They ran the entire distance. They didn't even stop in Bennet's kitchen to get something to eat. They went straight up to his bedroom, where, for the next hour and a half, they worked on the speech.

"Okay, Alva," said Pete finally. "Read me what we have so far." He lay on Bennet's bed, hands behind his head, staring up at the ceiling.

Bennet, seated at his desk, picked up the speech. He cleared his throat and began to read. "It's me again, with a few more words for my f-f-favorite governor. You say I'm a c-c-coward, Governor? Well, look who's t-t-talking! Y-y-your bark is worse than your bite! You talk about getting tough with criminals and yet y-y-you run off with your tail between your legs when it comes to getting tough on the things criminals use to commit crimes. G-g-guns! That's because if y-y-you got t-t-tough on guns, you'd have to get tough with the gun lobby! Y-y-you call me a coward, Governor, but I'll have you know, I've barked and chased after more d-d-dangerous int-t-truders than you'll ever know. So the next time you feel like calling somebody a big coward, look in the mirror, Governor, because you're nothing but a b-b-big puppy." (Bennet barked a couple of cute puppy barks.) "This is Deep Doo-doo, signing off."

Pete sat up and peered at Bennet. "Well, what do you think?"

"I-I-I think it sounds great," said Bennet.

Pete smiled. He looked pleased. "I do, too," he said. He hopped off the bed and, crouching, pulled out a large tape recorder, which Bennet kept under his bed. It was an ancient reel-to-reel that Bennet had purchased a long time ago at a tag sale for two dollars.

"Wh-what are you going to do with that?" asked Bennet.

"I want to record the speech," replied Pete. "We'll play it back at slow speed while we're broadcasting so my voice sounds deeper."

"You're being r-r-ridiculous," said Bennet. "Nobody knows it's you. Who cares how your voice sounds over the air?"

"*I* care!" declared Pete. "I don't want to sound like a woman."

"Nobody even knows it's you," said Bennet.

"It doesn't matter," replied Pete. "I don't want people thinking I'm a woman."

Bennet rolled his eyes.

• • •

At 5:15, Mr. Ordway got ready to go home from work. He was exhausted. It had been a long day, with many phone calls, meetings, and articles to write. Yet it had also been a very exciting day—an exhilarating day. After all, how often is it that a governor is interrupted on TV by a masked dog?

That morning when Mr. Ordway arrived at the newsroom, he showed Trombly, the managing editor of the North Agaming *Sun,* the note he had found on his windshield. Trombly stroked his beard as he studied the note carefully, wondering aloud if it was connected to last night's broadcast and if he should print it or not. He decided not to, though. "For all we know, it could just be a hoax," he said, handing the note back to Mr. Ordway.

Mr. Ordway put the note in his pocket. While he was pretty sure the note was not a hoax, he had no way to prove it wasn't. At the end of the day, briefcase in hand, Mr. Ordway said good-bye to

Jill, the reporter who sat next to him, and went out into the reception area. He pressed the down elevator button. When the elevator arrived, he stepped in and pushed the button for the first floor. As the elevator doors began to close, the door to the editorial room suddenly burst open and a young woman in an emerald-green dress ran to the elevator and stopped the doors from closing. It was Mary Geller, Trombly's secretary.

"Trombly wants you in his office, quick!" she cried.

"What's up?" asked Mr. Ordway as he stepped off the elevator.

"That mystery dog is on TV again," said Mary.

Mr. Ordway broke into a trot.

Trombly's office was filled with people. They were all squeezed in to watch the dog with the Dracula mask on the TV screen. The voice on TV sounded different from the first broadcast. It was deeper, for one thing, and slower. Clearly, the voice had been prerecorded on a tape recorder and was being played back at an abnormal speed. At one point, when the voice for the dog talked about chasing after intruders, a few people laughed, but they were immediately shushed by the others in the room, who wanted to hear every word that was said. After the broadcast ended, the entire room broke into applause. Grinning, Trombly put his arm around Mr. Ordway and said, "Well, Tom, your note said stay tuned and, sure enough, the dog returned. What's more, whoever is behind these broadcasts is now calling himself Deep Doo-doo—just like in your note. Looks like you've got yourself an anonymous source."

Deep Doo-doo
Strikes Again

Mr. Ordway returned to his desk, picked up the phone, and called home. He wanted to let Mrs. Ordway and Bennet know that he would be working late again tonight on account of this late-breaking Deep Doo-doo story. The phone answering machine picked up—which was strange because, while he knew his wife would still be at school, Bennet should have been home. He left a message on the machine, and then, turning on his computer, he began to write his story. He didn't take a break for a bite to eat or even for a cup of coffee. By 7:30, he had finished the story. He printed the story out, reread it a couple of times, and then walked across the newsroom to show Trombly.

Stevenson, the publisher, was in Trombly's office, so Mr. Ordway waited outside the door. Stevenson was a big man with a deep, booming voice. From where Mr. Ordway stood, he had no trouble hearing what Stevenson said.

"And I tell you, we're putting too much empha-sis on this Deep Doo-doo character," complained Stevenson, who was standing in front of Trombly's desk. "The governor's a good friend of mine. I don't want to embarrass him." With that, Mr. Ste-venson stormed out of the office, brushing past Mr. Ordway.

Mr. Ordway knocked on Trombly's door and walked in. "Stevenson giving you a hard time about all the stories we're running on Deep Doo-doo?" he asked.

"Yeah," grumbled Trombly. "The governor probably called and asked him to ease up on the news coverage. But that's my problem. Let's see what you've got."

Mr. Ordway handed him the story.

" 'Deep Doo-doo Calls Governor a Coward,' " said Trombly, reading the headline out loud. Mr. Ordway stood and watched as Trombly silently read the article. Finally, he looked up at Mr. Ord-way and said, "Let's go with it."

Twenty minutes later, Mr. Ordway stepped out of the building and into the cold, dark night. The parking lot was lighted by streetlamps. His car was parked by one of the newspaper delivery trucks. He walked over to it and started to open the driver's-side door when he heard a noise behind the delivery truck. Looking over, he saw nothing but darkness.

"Who's there?" Mr. Ordway called out.

Suddenly, from behind the truck, a small object flew out at him and dropped by his feet. It was a crumpled piece of paper. Mr. Ordway heard feet run off in the darkness. Mr. Ordway dashed after the person. He chased the person about a hundred yards or so—to the end of the parking lot—before he gave up. Whoever it was was a lot quicker on his feet than Mr. Ordway. Mr. Ordway walked back to his car. He searched in the dim light until he found the crumpled paper ball. He picked it up, smoothed it out, and stepped under a streetlamp to see if it held a message. It did:

*DEEP DOO-DOO
STRIKES AGAIN!*

Mr. Ordway didn't walk back into the building. He ran. He raced into the lobby and pushed the elevator button. When the elevator didn't open up right away, he opened the door to the building staircase and ran up the stairs—all three flights of them. He dashed through the newsroom and burst into Trombly's office, winded and looking very excited. Trombly stared at him in surprise. Mr. Ordway was panting so hard, he couldn't speak. He put the note on Trombly's desk, right under his nose. Trombly read the note. He didn't say a word to Mr. Ordway. He picked up the phone and called down to the pressroom. "Stop the presses!" he ordered. "We have a new lead story!"

• • •

That night each local TV station broke into its regularly scheduled broadcast to mention Deep Doo-doo's latest broadcast—with more details to follow on the eleven o'clock evening news. Channel 6, the station on which the two Deep Doo-doo broadcasts had appeared, canceled its usual programming to feature nonstop coverage of the Deep Doo-doo story. Not to be outdone, other channels also offered Deep Doo-doo specials. On Channel 9, for instance, a live call-in talk show devoted its entire hour to Deep Doo-doo, with one man calling in from as far away as British Columbia— where Deep Doo-doo's broadcast hadn't even been shown—to air his views. On Channel 25, a talk show host interviewed a panel of political experts, each of whom had a theory of who Deep Doo-doo might be.

"It's clearly someone in desperate need of psychological counseling," said the governor's campaign manager, a large, roundish man with a beard. "Only a sick mind would think of a such a thing."

The young man sitting beside him shook his head. He was the campaign manager for the other candidate. "I disagree with you, Jack," he said. "I think it's someone with a very clever mind who knows that the governor is vulnerable on a lot of issues."

"I think you're both overlooking the obvious," said a woman with short blond hair who was also part of the discussion panel. She was a political reporter for *Time* magazine. "For all we know, it could be someone who just adores dogs."

• • •

Mr. Ordway came home sometime after nine-thirty. Bennet and his mother were in the living room watching TV when Mr. Ordway walked in. He looked weary, with dark circles under his eyes. Yet, he also looked very happy. "Wait'll you hear what happened to me today," he said cheerfully, as he went into the kitchen to get himself a bottle of beer from the refrigerator. Mrs. Ordway got up to take his dinner out of the oven. She had saved him some chicken, which she and Bennet had had for dinner earlier that evening.

"Wh-wh-what happened?" asked Bennet when

his parents came back into the living room. His father wanted to eat his dinner in front of the big TV set.

"Deep Doo-doo contacted me," said Mr. Ordway.

"He contacted *you*?" said Mrs. Ordway incredulously as she set out his dinner on the coffee table.

"He left me a note," said Mr. Ordway. He tilted his head back and took a big swig of his beer.

"A note?" said Mrs. Ordway as she sat down on the couch beside her husband.

"Actually, two notes."

"When? Where? What did they say?" asked Mrs. Ordway.

Mr. Ordway laughed. He told Mrs. Ordway and Bennet about the notes and how he had written an article about them that was to appear on tomorrow's front page.

"How exciting!" said Mrs. Ordway.

Mr. Ordway beamed. "I'm on cloud nine," he said.

"Isn't it funny," said Mrs. Ordway. "And to think we were talking about anonymous sources just yesterday."

"I know it," said Mr. Ordway, laughing. He cut a piece of chicken with his knife and fork and put it in his mouth.

"Why do you suppose he contacted you?" asked Mrs. Ordway.

Mr. Ordway, his mouth full, shrugged. He swallowed and said, "I don't know. Maybe he likes what I write."

"Well, if that's the case, Deep Doo-doo's got good taste," said Mrs. Ordway.

"Shh-shh-shh!" said Mr. Ordway, pointing to the TV set.

A TV reporter was reporting live from outside the governor's mansion. "This just in from the governor's mansion," said the TV reporter, holding a microphone in his hand, speaking to the camera. "The governor in a written statement tonight said that he refuses to give credence to Deep Doo-doo by acknowledging these vicious attacks against his personal integrity."

"Oh, spare us," said Mr. Ordway.

The TV reporter went on, "Claiming that he's a victim of emotional terrorism, the governor has called a press conference for four o'clock tomorrow afternoon."

"Well, now," said Mr. Ordway. "Things are getting interesting."

The reporter continued, "According to the governor's office, the governor intends to show his deep concern for real issues by introducing his plan for health care at his press conference."

"Give me a break," said Mr. Ordway. "As if the governor really cares about the rising cost of health care. All he cares about are the rich. And they can afford any doctors they want."

Their eyes focused on the TV set, neither Mr. Ordway nor Mrs. Ordway noticed Bennet, seated in the rocking chair, take a ballpoint pen out of his pants pocket and scribble the numeral 4 on his palm.

Biggest News
Story of the Year

On a hunch, Trombly, the managing editor, had ordered an extra ten thousand papers printed up for the next day's edition. He had speculated that when word got out that Deep Doo-doo had communicated with one of his reporters, *The Sun* would sell like cold soda on a hot day at the ballpark. And that's just what happened. By the middle of the morning, you couldn't find a copy of *The Sun* for sale if your life depended on it. Trombly also had not told Stevenson about Deep Doo-doo getting in touch with Mr. Ordway. He knew that, being a friend of the governor's, the publisher would want to play down the story. Which is exactly what Stevenson tried to do.

"Why didn't anyone tell me Deep Doo-doo has been sending notes to Ordway?" thundered Stevenson as he burst into Trombly's office. Fuming, he clutched the morning edition in his hand and swirled it around in the air as though he were about to swat a fly. He slammed the door behind him and threw the paper down on Trombly's desk. It landed, front page up. DEEP DOO-DOO STRIKES AGAIN! roared the headline.

Trombly calmly looked up at Stevenson and said, "It happened last night after you left the office."

Stevenson said, "Well, you have my home telephone number. Why didn't you call?"

"There was no time to call. We had to go to press. This story was too big to hold up."

Stevenson's face grew red with anger. He looked as though he was about to say something that even his own paper would have been unable to print. Before he could speak—or, more likely, shout—there was a knock on the door. The door opened and Mary, Trombly's secretary, stuck her head in. She glanced warily over at Stevenson and then focused her eyes on Trombly. "Excuse me, Mr. Trombly," she said. "*The New York Times* is on line two."

"*The New York Times!*" bellowed Stevenson. "What do *they* want?"

"We've been receiving calls all morning," said Trombly. "Newspapers, magazines, TV stations, they're all calling us to find out more about Deep Doo-doo. In fact, Tom Ordway is being interviewed right this very minute by a reporter from

National Public Radio. I don't think you realize: This is the biggest news story of the year, and we've got the scoop on it. This little paper is going to be famous by the end of the day."

"It is?" said Stevenson, astonished, suddenly showing new interest—even delight. Although he was a friend of the governor's, he was also the publisher of the newspaper and, as publisher, he was responsible for its financial well-being. While the Deep Doo-doo story was bad news for the governor, it was good news for the paper. "Well, what are you waiting for?" demanded Stevenson. "Pick up the phone and talk to *The New York Times*."

Another Note

Mr. Ordway was having the biggest morning of his life. He was receiving phone calls from news reporters all over the country. He found himself in the media spotlight, and he was loving every minute of it. Every newspaper he had ever dreamed of working at—the *Los Angeles Times*, *The Miami Herald*, the *San Francisco Chronicle*, the *St. Louis Post-Dispatch*, the Atlanta *Journal & Constitution*, *The Philadelphia Inquirer*, *The Denver Post*, the *Chicago Sun-Times*, *The New York Times*, *The Boston Globe*, the *Seattle Post-Intelligencer*, the Minneapolis *Star Tribune*, even the legendary *Washington Post*—the paper that broke the Watergate story—called to ask him about Deep Doo-doo.

He also received calls from newspapers he'd never dreamed of working at—or had even heard of, for that matter. Papers like the Warwick, Rhode Island, *Beacon*; the Ellsworth, Maine, *American*;

the White River Junction, Vermont, *Valley News*; the Danville, Kentucky, *Advocate-Messenger*; the Fresno, California, *Bee*; and the Ashland, Oregon, *Daily Tidings*. As if that weren't sweet enough, Stevenson himself came by his desk and kindly put a hand on his shoulder and told him to keep up the good work. Yes, it was quite an exciting morning for Tom Ordway. But that was nothing compared to what happened at approximately twelve-thirty-five that afternoon when Jill handed him a fax that had just come in.

"What's this?" asked Mr. Ordway. "Not another newspaper request for an interview?"

"I'm not sure what to make of it, really," said Jill.

Mr. Ordway read the fax out loud. "Meet me at your car in ten minutes." Perplexed, Mr. Ordway stared at the fax, wondering who it was from. Then it clicked: The fax was from Deep Doo-doo. He sprang from his chair and dashed out to the elevator lobby. He ran down the stairs and out the building. He was all out of breath by the time he reached his car. There was nobody around. Suddenly he spied another note on his windshield wiper. Fingers trembling, heart racing, he unfolded the note.

STAY TUNED FOR
MY 4:00 PRESS CONFERENCE!
DEEP DOO-DOO

Mr. Ordway ran back into the building and showed the note to Trombly. Trombly read the note, then picked up the phone and called Stevenson.

"Sorry I'm late," said Stevenson a few minutes later when he walked into Trombly's office. "I was on the phone with *Newsweek*. What's up?"

"Another note," said Trombly.

Both Trombly and Mr. Ordway watched Stevenson read the note to himself. Finally, he looked up at them. "Has Deep Doo-doo contacted anyone else in the media about his press conference?"

"Not that we know," answered Trombly.

Stevenson could hardly control his excitement. "Well, what are we standing around for?" he demanded. "We can scoop everyone. Let's get an extra edition out before four o'clock!"

Show Time!

Bennet looked at his watch. It was four o'clock on the nose. Both he and Pete were in his living room, in front of the TV set. A TV anchorman was on the screen, talking about the governor's imminent press conference. "For those of you who just tuned in, let me recap the latest news developments. At approximately twelve-thirty today, Tom Ordway, a reporter at the North Agaming *Sun*, received another note from Deep Doo-doo, saying that he planned to hold a press conference at the same time that the governor was holding his. Let's go now to our political correspondent, Linda Kelly, who is standing outside the governor's mansion."

The TV screen cut to a woman dressed in a red coat standing on the front steps of the enormous governor's mansion, a classic example of Greek Revival architecture. "Linda," said the anchorman back at the station, "the governor must not be very

pleased about Deep Doo-doo calling a press conference at the same time as his own."

"To put it mildly, Scott," said the political correspondent into her microphone. "I'm told the
governor was furious when he heard the news. It
means he can't even go on TV anymore without
being interrupted by Deep Doo-doo. And there's
nothing he can do."

"Well, can't he cancel his press conference?"
asked the anchorman.

"The governor's political advisors discussed
that, Scott, but they were worried that if the
governor canceled his press conference, it would
only make the governor look weak in the eyes of
the voters. Don't forget he's already been labeled a
big puppy by Deep Doo-doo."

"So either way it's a no-win situation for the
governor," said the anchorman.

"It certainly appears that way for now," said the
political correspondent.

"Okay, thanks, Linda," said the anchorman as
the TV screen returned to the anchorman at his
desk. "I've just been told that the governor is
about to begin his press conference. So let's go to
the Blue Room of the governor's mansion, where
the governor has just entered."

Bennet rose from the couch, walked over to the TV set, and snapped it off. He looked at Pete and said, "I-i-it's *show time!*"

Bennet and Pete hurried upstairs to Bennet's bedroom, where they had left Gus tied to Bennet's bedpost. Gus rose to his feet when they walked in and, panting, wagged his tail.

Pete patted Gus on top of his head. "Ready for your big press conference, Gus?" he asked. Pete unstrapped the watch from his wrist and, squatting, attached it to Gus's left front leg, down by his paw.

Bennet, meantime, went to his bookcase and removed the screen lid on his gerbil aquarium. He reached into the aquarium and lifted out his two gerbils. He placed them in an old felt hat that he had found up in the attic and set the hat on the floor.

Bennet and Pete had spent the last few hours preparing for the press conference. They had skipped lunch so they could go to the school library and research health care. While at the library, they had stopped at the information desk to look at a special display of books on the environment. This gave them yet another issue to confront the governor on. Back at Bennet's house, Pete wrote a fast script for the press conference, and then he recorded it on the tape recorder. Bennet wanted to do a quick dress rehearsal, but there was no time.

"Y-y-you ready?" Bennet asked.

"I hope so," replied Pete. He crouched down to put on Gus's mask, but Gus wouldn't let him. The dog kept jerking his head.

Pete knew what to do, though. "Hey, Gus, look," he said, slipping the Frankenstein mask over his own face. "I'm wearing *my* mask."

It worked: Gus let him put on the mask. He even wagged his tail.

Bennet picked up the video camera off his desk and turned on the transmitter. Peering through the camera lens, he focused in on Gus's head. Then he pointed at Pete to begin. Pete reached over and flipped on the old tape recorder that was on Bennet's desk. It was already set at a slow speed.

"Hello, it's me again, Deep Doo-doo, being broadcast to you live," said Deep Doo-doo's deep, manly voice over the tape recorder. "I called this press conference today to talk about real issues, since you can bet your last dog biscuit the governor isn't going to talk about them at *his* press conference. Oh, sure, he may say he is, but, hey, he's the governor. He's like a Dalmatian: He can't change his spots. So let's begin. I've chosen two reporters out of a hat to ask me questions."

Bennet zoomed in on the two gerbils in the old felt hat.

The voice on the tape switched to a high, squeaky voice. "I have a question for you, Deep Doo-doo."

"Sorry, I didn't catch your name," said Deep Doo-doo's voice. Bennet zoomed in on Gus's masked face. As he filmed, he went from Gus to the gerbils, the gerbils to Gus, depending on whose voice was speaking on the tape recorder.

"I'm Sick," said the high, squeaky voice.

"And I'm Tired," said a much slower and tired-sounding voice.

"Sick and Tired," said Deep Doo-doo's voice. "Now what is your question, Sick?"

"I've noticed that you seem to pant a lot. Shouldn't you have that checked out?"

"You're absolutely right," said Deep Doo-doo's voice. "I should. But do you know how much it costs to see a veterinarian these days? It's ridiculous! But what's the governor doing about the rising cost of health care? Nothing! Nothing at all! That's because all he cares about are the rich! They don't have to worry about the high cost of health care. They can afford any doctors they want."

Standing just out of camera range, Pete lifted Gus's paw to make it look as though Gus was pointing to the other gerbil, the way a politician will do when he wants to take another reporter's question. "Yes, Tired."

"I have a question from a Great Dane who's visiting this part of the state. Can you recommend any good places to take a dog for a walk?"

"Well," said Deep Doo-doo's voice, "we have some very nice beaches. But you'd be wise to call ahead: They may be closed on account of all the junk that's washed up on shore. Contrary to what the governor says, he's hardly done a thing to clean up the beaches. And whatever you do, don't lap up the water. Next question. Yes, Tired."

"No, I'm Sick," said the high, squeaky voice.

"Sick, I'm just sick I thought you were Tired," said Deep Doo-doo's voice. "What's your question?"

"Why do you wear that scary mask?" asked the high, squeaky voice.

"Good question," said Deep Doo-doo's voice. "In fact, a good pal of mine, a golden retriever, asked me the very same thing not long ago. He said, 'Deep Doo-doo, why do you wear such a scary mask?' And do you know what I told him? I told him if you think this mask is scary, just look at all the scary things the governor is doing to our state."

Pete, off-camera, raised Gus's paw with the wristwatch to make it look as though he was examining his watch. "Well, I'm afraid that's all the time we have. This is Deep Doo-doo," Deep Doo-doo's prerecorded voice was saying when a very unexpected and unscripted thing happened: Gus leaped to his feet, knocking Pete over.

"Hey, Gus!" Pete cried out.

Luckily, he said it at the precise moment that Gus began to bark, drowning out his voice. Barking loudly, Gus knocked over the hat and took off after the two gerbils.

Startled, Bennet dropped the video camera. The camera lay on the floor and kept right on filming, for Bennet had locked the filming button. Bennet hopped over to the transmitter and yanked out the plug—but not before the camera recorded Gus in hot pursuit of the gerbils, chasing them under the bed.

A Hiatus

All three major TV networks showed excerpts of Deep Doo-doo's press conference on their evening newscasts. A blurred photograph taken at the end of the press conference, when the dog—now shown to be a black Labrador—was chasing after the two gerbils, Sick and Tired, made the front page of nearly every major newspaper in the country the next day. (PRESS CONFERENCE RUNS WILD, many of the headlines read.) One ambitious young reporter, hoping to reveal Deep Doo-doo's secret identity, went so far as to research the titles of every black Labrador registered in the state. Comedians on talk shows joked about the press conference ("You know you're in deep doo-doo when . . ."). And, somewhat surprisingly, there was even a rather admiring quote from the governor himself, who said he could think of a few reporters he'd like to go after the way Deep Doo-doo's dog went after those two reporters at the press conference.

The weekly supermarket tabloids were having a field day with Deep Doo-doo. (Being weeklies, they had already gone to press by the time of Deep Doo-doo's press conference.) Playing up the dog angle of the story, one tabloid claimed it was Elvis Presley himself, come back from the grave, reincarnated as a dog, who was wearing the Dracula mask. Another supermarket tabloid ran an exclusive interview with Maxine, the governor's collie, who told a woeful tail—as the tabloid put it—of neglect. "I bit the governor once and I'll bite him again," the collie was reported to have barked to her close friend, a maid at the governor's mansion who was in charge of feeding the dog.

After Deep Doo-doo's press conference, Mr. Ordway received a pile of hate mail from animal lovers criticizing Deep Doo-doo for allowing his dog to attack those two poor, defenseless little gerbils. Apparently, they thought Mr. Ordway had some way of getting in touch with Deep Doo-doo. They didn't realize that Mr. Ordway knew as much about Deep Doo-doo as they did. Anxious to find out more, Mr. Ordway began staying later and later at work. He called the phone number that was printed at the top of the fax that Deep Doo-doo had sent him—the phone number of the place from where it had been sent. It turned out that the message had been faxed from a stationery store in the West Hill section of town—not far from his own house. Mr. Ordway paid a visit to the stationery store. He questioned the woman behind the counter, but she was unable to tell him anything about the fax or who sent it. People are always coming in to send faxes, she told Mr. Ordway; how was she supposed to remember who sent what fax? Mr. Ordway also called the station manager at Channel 6 to ask if she had any thoughts on who Deep Doo-doo might be, but the station manager was of no help. And after Mr. Ordway thought about it, he realized why: Channel 6's ratings soared whenever Deep Doo-doo came on the air. The station wasn't about to help Mr. Ordway—or anyone, for that matter—pull the plug on Deep Doo-doo now. Trying a different approach, Mr. Ordway called an old engineering buddy from college whom he hadn't talked to in years and asked him what someone would need to do to interrupt a TV signal. His friend gave him a long, terribly technical answer that only a TV technician would have been able to fully comprehend. He did say, however, that a large antenna would be needed. Mr. Ordway called up every electronics store in the local yellow pages and asked if anyone had recently purchased a large antenna, but nothing came of that, either.

Mr. Ordway wasn't the only one who was putting in long hours on Deep Doo-doo. Since interfering with a television's broadcasting signal is a federal offense, the FCC, the Federal Communications Commission, was also trying to find out who Deep Doo-doo was. Agents from the FCC rode around in a van, trying to track down Deep Doo-doo's illegal signal on their mobile detection monitor. But whoever the perpetrator was—the one who called himself Deep Doo-doo—he was too clever: He never stayed on the air long enough to zero in on. At the governor's request, the Federal Bureau of Investigation was called in on the search. One afternoon an agent from the FBI came by the newspaper office to question Mr. Ordway about Deep Doo-doo. Citing his First Amendment rights—freedom of the press—Mr. Ordway refused to answer any of the agent's questions. Many other journalists were also pursuing the story, as were the local police. They all knew that whoever revealed Deep Doo-doo's identity first would receive great fame, not to mention a fat book contract.

• • •

Bennet was extremely shaken up after Deep Doo-doo's disastrous press conference. Just thinking about the press conference made him queasy. He shuddered every time he recalled the camera dropping from his hands. He was terrified that his mother or father would recognize his bedroom. But fortunately, from the clip Bennet saw later on TV, the camera had fallen so fast, it had made everything in his room a blur. As far as Bennet could tell, the only part of their secret that had been revealed was that Gus was a black Labrador.

To Bennet's surprise, Pete didn't seem the least bit fazed by the press conference. In fact, he thought it was funny. This not only baffled Bennet; it annoyed him. How could Pete be so unconcerned over the possibility of getting caught? Pete didn't even scold Gus for being a bad dog.

The afternoon after the press conference Bennet and Pete looked for another tall tree to put the antenna in, one farther away from his house. Now that the trees were starting to lose their leaves, Bennet was worried that someone might see the antenna from the street and become suspicious.

With Gus at his heels, Pete stepped up to a large birch tree that stood near the corner of the Ordways' backyard. The tree shimmered with golden yellow leaves. "How about this tree?" he asked as Gus sniffed the trunk of the tree.

Bennet shook his head and said, "It's too c-c-colorful. My m-m-mom might look at that tree."

"Well, then," said Pete, walking over to a gigantic spruce tree that was growing near Mr. Ordway's small vegetable garden. The garden still had cornstalks from the summer, which were now brown and withered. "How about this tree?"

"It's too small," said Bennet.

Pete gazed up at the tree, saying, "You call this small?"

Pete suggested several other trees, none of which met Bennet's approval. Finally, Pete said, "Look, what's the problem?"

"What d-d-do you mean?" replied Bennet, without looking over.

"You know what I mean," said Pete. "Something's bugging you."

Bennet turned and gave Pete the most penetrating glare. "All right," he said. "I-I-I'll tell you what's b-b-bugging me. I'm upset about the press conference! We never should have done that p-p-press conference! It was a stupid idea."

"Hey, it was your idea, too."

"No, it wasn't," said Bennet. "I just wanted

t-t-to do a regular broadcast. You wanted to do a p-p-press conference."

"Well, it was a great idea," said Pete. "You said so yourself."

"Yeah—before it b-b-backfired. You could've gotten us caught."

"*Me?*" said Pete.

"Well, it was y-y-your idea—and *your* dog!"

"Hey, leave Gus out of this," said Pete, tying to keep his cool.

"How c-c-can I?" said Bennet. "Now everyone knows it's Gus."

"They just know it's a black Lab," said Pete, trying to calm Bennet down. "You know how many black Labs there are? Thousands! Maybe even millions! Listen," he went on. "You're just nervous. Don't worry. Nothing is going to happen."

"How d-d-do you know?"

"Because it would've happened by now."

"You think so?" said Bennet. He was feeling a little better, now that he had said what was on his mind.

"Yes, I do," said Pete. "Now here's what I think we should do. I think we should have Deep Doo-doo take a hiatus. Until things settle down."

"That's p-p-probably not a bad idea," agreed Bennet.

"It's a great idea," said Pete. "I only come up with great ideas. Now c'mon, let's pick a tree—no, *you* pick a tree."

The tree Bennet selected was in the woods just beyond the stone wall that ran along the edge of his backyard. The tree was so far away from Bennet's bedroom window that more antenna wire was needed in order to hook the antenna up to the transmitter. That meant another trip to B & G's Hardware.

"Well, hello, strangers," said Jimmy when they walked in through the door. "Long time no see."

Bennet was about to say hello when he noticed a button pinned to the front pocket of Jimmy's plaid shirt. The button featured a dog's head wearing a Dracula mask. "Hey," said Bennet. "Wh-wh-where did you get the b-b-button?"

Jimmy touched the button. "Some guy was selling them on the sidewalk," he replied. "He had all kinds of Deep Doo-doo stuff. Buttons, bumper stickers, T-shirts."

"Really? T-shirts?" said Pete.

"Wh-wh-what do you think of this Deep Doo-doo?" asked Bennet.

"I think he's great," said Jimmy.

"Did you see his press conference?" asked Pete.

"Most exciting press conference I've ever seen," said Jimmy. "I particularly liked the way that dog went after those two rodents. Man, I could sure use a dog like that down in my cellar. So, fellas, what can I do for you?"

"We need to buy antenna wire," said Pete.

"Actually," said Bennet, who knew more about antennas than Pete, "we need to buy coaxial cable." He was thinking that, given the extra distance of the antenna, a better-quality antenna connection was in order. It would help prevent signal loss.

"How much cable do you need?" asked Jimmy as the three of them walked down the aisle where the antenna items were located.

"A lot," said Bennet.

Jimmy pointed to several different packages of gray, coiled cable that were hanging from hooks along the wall. "You have a choice. Twenty-five feet. Fifty feet. And a hundred feet. Or we have it by the spool."

Pete looked at Bennet. "How much do you figure we need?"

Bennet tried to estimate the amount in his head. "I-I-I'd say about two hundred feet."

Jimmy whistled. "That *is* a lot of cable. Let's see, two hundred feet of coaxial cable comes to . . .

twenty-six dollars and thirty-four cents with tax."

"On second thought," said Bennet, "we'll j-j-just get a hundred yards of regular old three-hundred-ohm b-b-brown, flat antenna wire."

"Tell you what," said Jimmy. "I'm getting a big shipment of inventory in about two weeks. If you'll help me stock it, I'll give you two hundred feet of coaxial cable, plus we'll forget all about the money you owe me. We'll call it an even swap."

Pete's eyes glistened. "Sounds good to me," he said.

"Sounds good to me, too," said Bennet.

"So we got a deal?" asked Jimmy.

Bennet and Pete said together, "We got a deal."

Jimmy put the cable in a bag for them. As Bennet and Pete were leaving the store, Jimmy called out, "Don't forget to tell your friends about us."

Another Job for Deep Doo-doo

Around this time a poll was conducted among voters in the state and a curious phenomenon was discovered: Since Deep Doo-doo's first TV broadcast, the governor's popularity had plummeted. According to this most recent poll, the governor had slipped forty-two percentage points in popularity—only thirty-five percent of the registered voters planned to vote for him. The poll, which appeared under a headline that said GOV IN REAL TROUBLE ON REAL ISSUES! found that the governor's race was now dead even, a toss-up, between the governor and his challenger. The governor was understandably very troubled by his latest standing in the polls. On the advice of his political advisors, the governor began to vigorously attack Deep Doo-doo in his speeches. What else could he do? He had already portrayed himself as a victim, and that hadn't worked. So he lashed out at Deep Doo-doo, demanding that he stop hiding behind that dog. GOV TO MASKED CANINE: CAN IT!

screamed one newspaper headline after a particularly fiery speech that the governor gave on the steps of the governor's mansion—a speech, incidentally, that was barred to television cameras for fear that if it appeared on TV, Deep Doo-doo would only interrupt it. Yet, despite all the governor's efforts, despite a photograph that the governor's people released to the press showing the governor being licked on the face by a cuddly Newfoundland puppy, the governor continued to slip in the polls. One reason for that, political experts agreed, was that, by attacking Deep Doo-doo, the governor was still avoiding any talk about real issues. (GOV DOGGED BY REAL ISSUES! cried one headline.) Another reason for the the governor's sinking popularity was that people genuinely liked Deep Doo-doo, and they didn't like the governor attacking him.

It was as simple as that.

• • •

For nearly a week, Bennet and Pete kept off the air. This was Bennet's doing: He was uncomfortable about broadcasting again. If it had been up to Pete, they would have broadcast again in a second. Pete did everything he could think of to allay Bennet's fears and change his mind. He told Bennet what a shame it was that his broadcasting ingenuity should go to waste. He told him how unfair it was to deprive people of their favorite TV personality, Deep Doo-doo. He also pointed out to Bennet, again and again, that their broadcasting days were numbered. The campaign was in its final stage. Election Day was next Tuesday. After Tuesday, there would be no reason for Deep Doo-doo to appear on TV. Pete even went so far as to purchase a newspaper each morning on their way to school so he could read articles about the governor to Bennet while they were eating their lunch. He hoped that one of the articles might spark a fuse in Bennet, inciting him to action.

"You should read this article your dad wrote," said Pete, looking up from the newspaper that he had spread out on the table. He and Bennet had the whole table to themselves. The cafeteria was nearly empty. Most of the other students, having finished their lunches, had gone outside to the playground.

"Why? Wh-wh-what's my dad say?" asked Bennet. Reaching over, he picked up his half pint–size carton of milk. He put the plastic straw to his lips and took a sip.

"Your and my favorite governor is attending a fund-raising dinner tomorrow night."

"He is?" said Bennet.

"Guess how much it costs to attend?" said Pete.

"How much?"

"One thousand dollars a plate!"

Bennet opened his eyes wide in amazement. "A thousand dollars a p-p-plate?" he said. "You're k-k-kidding!"

"No," said Pete. "The money is going to the governor's reelection campaign. You know what I think?"

Bennet picked up a string bean and put it in his mouth. "What?"

"This is another job for . . ." Pete put his fist to his mouth and pretended to blow a trumpet. He made a trumpetlike sound, a call to arms. "Deep Doo-doo!"

"I-I-I don't know if that's such a good idea," said Bennet.

"Why not?" asked Pete.

"Well, f-f-for one thing," said Bennet, "I-I-I'm worried Gus might go crazy again. Like at the p-p-press conference."

Pete dismissed this worry with a wave of his hand. "Forget the press conference. That's ancient history," he said. "If it wasn't for those gerbils of yours, Gus never would've acted that way."

"Y-y-you make it sound as if it was all their fault."

"Well, it was," said Pete.

"It was not!" protested Bennet.

"Tell you what," said Pete. "We'll put the gerbils in another room when we broadcast again. That way Gus won't get excited."

"I-I-I still don't know," said Bennet.

"You should read your dad's article," said Pete. "He talks all about fund-raising dinners and campaign contributions and why there should be a limit on what people can contribute."

"Why should there be?" asked Bennet.

Pete picked up his fork and pointed the prongs at Bennet. "Let's pretend you're the governor and I'm Joe Schmo, okay?"

Bennet smiled. "Okay, Joe."

"Now. Here we are at our big fund-raising luncheon that I've just paid one thousand dollars—"

"One thousand dollars to eat meat loaf that tastes like cardboard!" cried Bennet, appalled, pushing his plate away. "Y-y-you're out of your mind!"

"Pretend it's roast beef," said Pete.

"Not the cafeteria's roast b-b-beef that tastes like leather!"

"No, *real* roast beef," said Pete, growing impatient. "Anyway. Say there's a law that has come up that needs your signature." He glanced around at the mostly empty tables. He saw pretty Sally Pickert two tables away. She was sitting with her best friend, Alison Katz. "Say Sally Pickert wants to paint the cafeteria walls bright purple—"

"Purple!" exclaimed Bennet, making a face.

"Yeah, purple," said Pete. "And I want to paint them green. She hasn't contributed one penny to your reelection campaign, while I've paid a thousand dollars for the honor of sitting in your presence. Now what color are you going to let the cafeteria walls be painted—purple, the color Sally wants—or green, the color I want?"

"That's easy," said Bennet. "Purple."

"Purple!" cried Pete in disbelief. "You would not!"

"I would t-t-too!"

"But I contributed all that money to help you be reelected!" said Pete.

"Yeah, b-b-but Sally Pickert is pretty," said Bennet. "And I'll do anything to make her happy."

Pete rolled his eyes. "Well, you see my point, right?"

"I-I-I do," said Bennet.

"So what do you say?"

"This looks like another job for Deep Doo-doo," said Bennet.

Pete smiled. He took his spiral-bound notebook and a pen out of his backpack. He opened the notebook and, pen poised, looked over at Bennet and said, "I know exactly what Deep Doo-doo should say."

"Just as long as we d-d-don't do another p-p-press conference," said Bennet.

"We won't," Pete assured him. "This is going to be even better. This is going to be—"

"Stup-p-pendous!" broke in Bennet.

"Magnificent!"

"Unf-f-forgettable!"

Deep Doo-doo's
Fund-Raising Dinner

Mr. Ordway couldn't understand what had become of Deep Doo-doo. He hadn't heard from Deep Doo-doo since his press conference, and that was almost a week ago. Mr. Ordway hoped nothing terrible had happened to whoever was behind Deep Doo-doo—or his dog. He hoped the dog hadn't run away or, worse, been hit by a car. Maybe the dog really did have some sort of health problem, as was suggested at the press conference. But then again, there was always the possibility that Deep Doo-doo had decided to call it quits after the dog's press conference. All Mr. Ordway could do was wonder, and wait.

Mr. Ordway's waiting ended one afternoon at work, just a few days before the election. He had been working on an article for the next day's edition—an article about the governor's troubles at the polls—when he decided to take a break and get a cup of coffee from the diner across the street. He was walking toward the elevators when the receptionist, who had started only a few days ago, stopped him. "Someone called and left a message for you," she said. The receptionist handed Mr. Ordway a pink slip of paper on which she had scribbled the message. "He didn't say who he was."

Mr. Ordway stared at the small piece of paper. The message simply said: "We strike again at 4:30." Nothing else. Mr. Ordway looked at the receptionist. "When did this come in?" he asked.

The receptionist shrugged. "Oh, I don't know. Around one o'clock or so."

"One o'clock!" exclaimed Mr. Ordway. "That's over three hours ago! Do you know who this is from?" he demanded. He was trying not to lose his temper.

"The person didn't say," said the receptionist.

"It's from Deep Doo-doo!" cried Mr. Ordway.

The receptionist looked astonished. "It is?"

"Why didn't you tell me I had a message?" demanded Mr. Ordway. "We could've printed an extra edition!"

"Well, I didn't know it was from Deep Doo-doo," said the receptionist, becoming rather huffy. "It's not like he said who he was or anything. I mean, *really*! He should've told me he was Deep Doo-doo. But all he said was, 'We strike again at four-thirty.' For all I knew, it was your garbageman. Those garbagemen are always going on strike."

Mr. Ordway let it drop. He looked at his wristwatch. It was almost four-thirty now. He turned and hustled back into the newsroom.

"Hey, everyone, Deep Doo-doo is on TV," he shouted as he ran through the newsroom to Trombly's office. Deep Doo-doo had become a kind of celebrity within the office—indeed, almost a folk hero. Mr. Ordway knew they would all want to see the dog on TV.

"What do you mean Deep Doo-doo is on TV?" cried Trombly when Mr. Ordway entered his office.

"He left a message for me that said he's going to strike again at four-thirty," said Mr. Ordway.

Stevenson entered the room. "What's this I hear about Deep Doo-doo being on TV?" he demanded.

"He left me another note," said Mr. Ordway.

Stevenson examined his wristwatch. "Why didn't Deep Doo-doo tell us sooner? We could've put out an extra edition!"

Mr. Ordway didn't tell Stevenson that Deep Doo-doo's message had been sitting out on the new receptionist's desk for the past three hours. He knew it would only get her in trouble. "Must be something urgent," was all he said.

Trombly's office was rapidly filling up with people. All eyes focused on the small TV screen on the bookcase. A rerun of *Gilligan's Island* was on. The shipwrecked crew was on a beach waving like maniacs to a distant ocean liner.

"Oh, this is one of my favorite episodes," said Beverly De Jong, the drama and movie critic for the paper.

Suddenly the TV lost its signal. For a moment, the picture became scrambled. Then there was a bright flash and the familiar dog appeared, wearing his now infamous Dracula mask.

"Look, there's the dog!" cried Jill, pointing to the TV.

Deep Doo-doo began to speak in his distinctive deep voice. "Hello, I'm Deep Doo-doo. As many of you know, the governor is having a one-thousand-dollar-a-plate dinner tonight to help pay for his reelection bid. Well, I'd like to tell you about my own fund-raising dinner. That's right. I'm having a one-thousand-dollar-a-bowl-of-dog-food dinner. All my supporters will be there—cocker spaniels, springer spaniels, fox terriers, Dalmatians, German shepherds, dachshunds, greyhounds, even Doberman pinschers. They'll all be there because they all want me to push their pet causes. Like providing shelters for stray dogs. Now perhaps one of you out there has some special interest you'd like me to push. Well, if you don't mind leftovers for dinner, come join us at my one-thousand-dollar-a-bowl-of-dog-food-fund-raising dinner. And now for a commercial interruption."

Trombly, who was standing, arms folded, beside Mr. Ordway, turned to Mr. Ordway with a quizzical expression on his face. "Deep Doo-doo has a commercial?" he asked. Apparently, he considered Mr. Ordway an expert on Deep Doo-doo.

Mr. Ordway could only shrug and say, "I guess so."

The TV cut to the dog's paw. There was a package of strange-looking screws attached to the dog's paw with Scotch tape.

"I ask you," continued Deep Doo-doo's voice, offscreen. "How much would you expect to pay for these toggle screws? A dollar forty-nine? A dollar twenty-nine?"

Trombly murmured, "A dollar forty-nine."

"Try eighty-nine cents!" said Deep Doo-doo.

"Eighty-nine cents!" blurted Trombly in amazement. "Impossible!"

"Yes," said Deep Doo-doo. "Just eighty-nine cents! That's how much toggle screws cost at B & G's Hardware store. The fact is, everything costs less at B & G's. Sandpaper. Tools. Paints. Nuts. Bolts. You name it. See this socket wrench?" The camera zoomed in on a socket wrench. "At any other hardware store, this socket wrench would run you five, six, maybe even seven dollars. But at B & G's it's only a dollar ninety-nine! That's right. Only a dollar ninety-nine! Of course, don't expect to find the governor shopping at B & G's. That's because B & G's is located on Broad Street, where most of the stores are boarded up and most of the people who live in the area can't find jobs. The governor would rather you forget all about places like Broad Street. That's why you only see him in front of a big American flag. But, Governor, I have news for you: That American flag you probably paid fifty bucks for costs less than twenty bucks at B & G's! So if you know how to spend your hard-earned money better than the governor knows how to spend our tax dollars, get on down to B & G's Hardware!"

The TV set became scrambled again. A second later, *Gilligan's Island* came back on the screen.

Trombly turned to Mr. Ordway and said,

"Quick, Ordway, get down to B & G's Hardware and check this story out." He reached into his back pocket and pulled out his wallet. He removed a couple of singles. "And while you're there, pick me up a few toggle screws."

The Phone Call

Bennet and Pete had no sooner gone off the air when they were out the door and on their way to B & G's Hardware. They were elated, even giddy. They were like two actors who've just stepped off a stage after giving the performance of their lives.

"I hope Jimmy saw it," said Pete.

"M-m-me too," said Bennet.

"Well, if he didn't, at least he'll hear about it on the news," said Pete.

"You d-d-don't think we went t-t-too far this time, do you, Pete?" asked Bennet.

Pete shook his head. "No way."

Reassured, Bennet said, "Hey, I know. When we see Jimmy, let's p-p-pretend we know nothing about the b-b-broadcast. Let's act real surprised when he t-t-tells us."

"No, no, no," said Pete excitedly. "Let's say we just heard on the radio that Channel Six is angry about the free commercial for B & G's Hardware.

Let's say they want B & G's Hardware to pay for the commercial."

"That's a t-t-terrific idea!" said Bennet.

"I can't wait to see the look on his face when we tell him," said Pete. "So tell me. Have I made up for the press conference?"

"You've red-d-deemed yourself," said Bennet.

They crossed Sagamore Street and then took the shortcut behind the Grand Union to Franklin Avenue. They followed Franklin for a few blocks and turned down Jackson Street, where all the car dealerships and fast-food restaurants were located. Then they turned down Windsor Street—the street the old Mead place was on. As they hurried along Windsor Street, three police cars raced by with their lights blazing, their sirens wailing. Bennet and Pete thought nothing of it, though: They just figured it was a fire or an accident or something.

But then, as they turned down Broad Street, Bennet and Pete saw an enormous crowd gathered in front of B & G's Hardware. There must have been at least a hundred people. Police cars, their red and blue lights flashing, were parked up and down the street. Police officers were scurrying about, trying to keep the crowd under control. TV news teams were on the scene, and several TV reporters were already broadcasting live in front of the hardware store.

Bennet panicked. Without saying a word, he took a step backward, turned, and began to sprint down the sidewalk.

"Hey, Alva, wait!" shouted Pete. He tore after him. He caught up to Bennet and, grabbing him by the back of his sweatshirt, forced him to stop. "Stop, will ya!" he cried, breathing hard. Pete's face was flushed and sweaty. "What are you, crazy? You're going to get us caught!"

"W-w-we've got to g-g-get out of here!" insisted Bennet, panting for breath.

"Not by running, we don't," said Pete. "We'll walk—slowly—so we don't attract attention."

"D-d-do you th-think anyone saw us?" asked Bennet as he started to walk.

"I don't know," answered Pete. He turned and peered behind him. "Wow! Look at all those cops!"

"I-I-I d-d-don't want to look," said Bennet. "I j-j-just want to go home and p-pray nothing more happens."

• • •

Bennet was unusually quiet at dinner that evening. And he didn't have much of an appetite. He only picked at his food, even though it was lasagna, his favorite meal. He was worried sick about what he had seen that afternoon in front of B & G's Hardware. Clearly, he and Pete had gone too far with Deep Doo-doo's commercial for B & G's Hardware. Why did he ever let Pete talk him into running a TV commercial? He should've known it would only bring the police to B & G's. Bennet hoped he and Pete hadn't gotten Jimmy in any sort of trouble.

"Is everything okay, dear?" asked his mother, who was sitting across the table from him. The little TV set by the kitchen table was on. As usual, it was turned to the news. A scholarly looking man with glasses, the station's news analyst, was giving a commentary on the governor's race, trying to put the whole thing into perspective.

"Wh-wh-why d-d-do you ask?" asked Bennet.

"You seem upset about something."

"I-I-I'm not upset."

"You sure?"

"P-p-positive."

Mrs. Ordway sighed. "I'll be so glad when this election is over and we see more of your father." Mr. Ordway was working late again that night.

Just then, the phone rang. Usually Bennet, who sat closest to the phone, which was on the wall by the refrigerator, answered the phone when it rang during dinner. But not tonight. Tonight he made no effort to answer it. His mother gave him a strange look as she rose to get it. "Hello?" she said. Mrs. Ordway listened. ". . . Yes, he's here. Who's this?"

Bennet's heart nearly exploded. Someone was calling him? *Who?* It wasn't Pete, because his mother knew Pete. Who could it be? The police? His mother handed him the phone, saying, "It's someone named Jimmy."

"Oh," said Bennet, relieved, rising from his chair. Then he became scared. *Why was Jimmy calling him? And at this hour?* He put the receiver to his ear and, in a whisper-thin voice, said, "H-h-hello?"

"Bennet, this is Jimmy." It sounded like he was talking from an outdoor pay telephone. Cars were swishing by in the background. "I've been racking my brain trying to think who I know who'd be capable of putting out a TV broadcast. Then I thought of you and Pete. I just have this to say, Bennet: Be careful. Both the police and FBI—"

"Th-th-the *who*?" said Bennet, shocked.

"The FBI," said Jimmy. "The police and FBI were at the store today asking me a lot of questions about today's Deep Doo-doo broadcast. I didn't tell them anything. So don't worry. But be careful, okay?"

Bennet suddenly felt weak. He leaned against the refrigerator to steady himself. The FBI was after him and Pete! *The FBI!* "Okay," was all he could manage to say.

"I don't want to see you boys get in trouble," Jimmy went on. Then he joked, "After all, I need you to help me with my inventory."

Bennet did not laugh. "J-j-jimmy," he said.

"Yes?"

Bennet blanked out for a moment. He couldn't remember what he was going to say. He was still thinking about the FBI. A feeling of dread crept over him as he began to realize all the trouble he and Pete were in.

"Bennet?" he heard Jimmy say.

Bennet was going to tell Jimmy how sorry he was for any trouble he and Pete had caused him, but a glance over at his mother told him not to. Although she was sitting at the kitchen table with her eyes on the small TV set, he knew she was listening closely. "I-I-I'll see you later," said Bennet.

"You be careful now, you hear?"

The moment Bennet hung up the phone, his mother said, "Who was that?"

"J-j-jimmy," replied Bennet.

"Jimmy who?"

"J-jimmy over at B-B-B & G's Hardware."

"Why on earth was he calling you?"

"To t-t-tell me that some switches P-p-pete and I ordered had c-c-come in."

"He's calling you at this hour just to tell you *that*?" said Mrs. Ordway, astonished. She knew Bennet shopped at B & G's—now she understood why. "I guess that Deep Doo-doo is right. B & G's Hardware is special. Did your friend Jimmy say anything about Deep Doo-doo?"

"No."

His mother gave him a peculiar look. She made Bennet very uneasy. "Are you sure you're okay?" she asked. "You look white as a ghost."

"I'm fine," said Bennet. "C-c-can I be excused from the t-t-table?"

"But you've hardly eaten anything!"

"I w-w-want to tell P-p-pete that our switches are in," said Bennet.

Bennet hurried upstairs to his parents' bedroom and closed the door behind him. He picked up the phone on the table by his parents' bed. He was so nervous, his fingers trembled. He kept pushing the wrong buttons as he tried to dial Pete's number. He had to hang up and start over four times. But it was urgent that he talk to Pete. It was more than urgent: It was a matter of life or prison. He had to tell Pete about the FBI and that Jimmy knew who Deep Doo-doo was and that they had to get rid of the transmitter—as soon as possible.

As Bennet stood there, arms folded, listening to Pete's phone ring, he gazed out his parents' bedroom window. It was dark outside, and the streetlamps on the telephone poles were lighted. Focusing his eyes on the cars parked along the street, Bennet became aware of one car in particular, a green sedan, that was sitting in front of his house by a telephone pole. Bennet leaned close to the windowpane, straining to see the car better. He gasped. There was a dark figure of a man in the front seat!

Someone was watching his house!

"Hello? Hello?" a girl's voice squirmed on the other end of the wire. It was Pete's older sister, Emma.

Bennet slammed down the phone. He was terrified that his phone was being bugged.

A Horrible Discovery

The next day, Saturday, Mr. Ordway went in to work. He didn't usually work on Saturdays, which helps to explain why, when he announced his plans at breakfast that morning, Mrs. Ordway lost her temper. Bennet, who hated it when his parents fought, got up from the kitchen table and left the room.

As he walked upstairs, he heard his mother shout: "Why don't you just sleep at the office? You practically live there as it is, anyway! Nothing is getting done around the house. The leaves on the lawn need raking. The storm windows need to be put up. You promised me months ago that you'd spackle that crack on Bennet's bedroom wall and you still haven't done it."

When Bennet reached the second floor, he walked right past his bedroom. He continued to the end of the hallway and entered his parents' bedroom. Their large bed was still unmade. Being careful not to walk in front of the window that faced the street, Bennet slipped over to the wall. He pressed his back against the wall and edged close to the window. His heart thumped as he pulled the curtain slightly away. Holding his breath, he peeked out.

The green sedan was still parked in front of his house.

• • •

Mr. Ordway knew his wife had every reason to be angry at him. He was angry at himself for spending so much time at the office. But he couldn't help it. He was obsessed with finding out who Deep Doo-doo was. He was even losing sleep over it. Just last night he had lain awake in bed for hours thinking about the notes that Deep Doo-doo had sent him. He had studied the notes so often, he had them memorized. One thing that always puzzled Mr. Ordway was why, of all the many reporters Deep Doo-doo could have communicated with, he chose him, a small-city newspaper reporter nobody had ever heard of. But something else was troubling Mr. Ordway. He couldn't quite put his finger on what it was, exactly, but he knew it had to do with one of Deep Doo-doo's broadcasts, the press conference broadcast.

Although it was Saturday, and although Trombly and much of the staff were off for the weekend, the newsroom was humming with activity as the rest of the employees went about putting out the Sunday edition. Mr. Ordway entered Trombly's darkened office and flicked on the lights. He stepped over to the bookcase where Trombly kept a collection of VCR tapes of important televised news events. The tapes lined a shelf, alongside a VCR machine. Each cassette was in its own plastic case, and each plastic case was marked on its binding. He pulled out the tape that said "Deep Doo-doo—Press Conference." He opened the case and slipped the cassette into the VCR machine. He pushed the PLAY button and sat down at Trombly's desk. He watched the tape from start to finish; then he got up and rewound the tape and played it again. As he was watching it a second time, Liz Dolan, the fashion editor, walked past the doorway and glanced into the office.

"Oh, you're watching the Deep Doo-doo press conference!" she cried with delight as she shuffled into the office. Liz pulled up a chair and sat down to watch, too. Apparently, she was a big fan of Deep Doo-doo.

Mr. Ordway's eyes remained fixed on the TV screen. He was looking for clues.

"Oh, here comes the part where Deep Doo-

doo's dog goes after Sick and Tired," said Liz, who seemed to know the press conference by heart. "There he goes!" she cried, laughing, as the black Labrador jumped up and the camera fell to the floor.

"Rewind that part!" Mr. Ordway suddenly blurted out.

Liz leaned forward and pushed the button on the VCR that rewound the tape. It had only just begun to rewind when Mr. Ordway said, "Okay, stop the tape and push Play."

Liz followed his directions.

"Slow it down," ordered Mr. Ordway. His gaze never left the TV.

Liz pressed the button that put the tape in slow motion. On the TV screen, the dog—a black blur —began to move at glacier speed. Liz glanced over at Mr. Ordway and said, "You're really into this, aren't you?"

Mr. Ordway didn't hear a word she said. He was hoping—praying—that he hadn't seen what he thought he'd just spotted. "Get ready to stop the tape," he said. He held up his hand. "Okay," he said, his eyes on the TV screen. "Stop it riiiiiiight . . . *here*!" He pointed to the TV screen.

Liz put the VCR machine on pause, and the image on the TV screen froze. The image was of a wall, shot at a crooked angle from the floor.

Liz, leaning forward, squinted her eyes at the out-of-focus TV screen. "Is that a crack, on the wall?" she asked.

Mr. Ordway didn't answer. He was staring at the TV screen in horror. He had just made a horrible, horrible discovery. It was a crack, all right—it was the *S*-shaped crack by the radiator in Bennet's bedroom, the one his wife had been nagging him for months to patch.

Mr. Ordway sighed. "Okay," he said, sinking into his chair. "Let's see the rest of the tape."

Liz reached down and pushed the PLAY button. The tape continued to play at normal speed. When the two gerbils appeared in the felt hat, Mr. Ordway suddenly realized that he was staring at his own hat—the hat he used to wear when he was a college student. He still had the hat, though he never wore it anymore. He kept it up in the attic.

"Poor Sick and Tired!" wailed Liz as the tape showed the dog chasing them under the bed. "Sick and Tired," she said with a laugh. "What great names!" She looked at Mr. Ordway and added, "You know, whoever this Deep Doo-doo is, he has the same wacky sense of humor as you."

Yes or No

While Mr. Ordway was busy at his office, searching for evidence, Bennet and Pete were also busy, destroying evidence. Bennet was in a state of near hysteria: He couldn't believe the green sedan was still parked in front of his house. Pete did his best to calm Bennet. "It's probably just some guy whose car broke down," Pete said as he helped Bennet take apart the transmitter.

"I-I-I'm t-t-telling you, it's an undercover cop," whispered Bennet. He was whispering in case his room was being bugged. He also had his radio turned on, loud, to drown out his and Pete's voices. Bennet removed the screws on the back of the transmitter with his Swiss army knife. Then, using a pair of long-nosed pliers, he began pulling apart the guts of the transmitter. As frightened as he was, Bennet was unable to bring himself to toss everything out. He salvaged all the parts he thought he could use for future projects. After Bennet had dismantled the transmitter, he and

Pete erased every Deep Doo-doo tape Pete had made on the old tape recorder. They cut the tapes up into little pieces and threw the pieces and the transmitter parts into several green plastic garbage bags. The plan was to dump the garbage bags in different locations around town. Bennet and Pete wanted to make it almost impossible to trace any of the evidence back to them. There was only one problem: Bennet's mother was downstairs. There was no way they could carry the garbage bags out of the house without her seeing them.

"We'll just have to go out your window," said Pete.

"B-b-but if we go out the w-w-window, that guy in the g-g-green car will see us," said Bennet.

"Yeah, you're right," said Pete. He snapped his fingers. "I know what we'll do. You go out to the street and—"

"You w-w-want me to *what*?" cried Bennet.

"Go out to the street," said Pete. "I need you to create a diversion so the guy won't see me sneak out of the window with the garbage bags."

"Wh-wh-what kind of a d-d-diversion?" asked Bennet.

"I don't know. Ask him for directions."

Bennet said, *"Directions?"*

"Yeah, pretend you're lost."

"You really think that'll w-w-work?"

Pete shrugged. "If it doesn't, maybe they'll let us share the same jail cell."

Bennet was too nervous to laugh. Slipping downstairs, he opened the front door and stepped outside. The moment Bennet looked over at the green sedan, he knew he didn't have the courage to ask the man for directions. Fortunately, he thought of something else he could do. He walked into his garage and went to the shelf that held all the sporting goods. He took down the football that his father had given to him for his birthday last year. The football was used so infrequently, it was slightly deflated. Bennet wandered out onto the street, tossing the football up over his head and catching it.

Just as Bennet hoped, the man in the green sedan looked over. He was wearing sunglasses. Of course he'd have on sunglasses, thought Bennet. *All* undercover cops wear sunglasses.

As Bennet tossed the football to himself, he glanced over at his house. He saw Pete crawl out of his bedroom window. Once outside on the small roof, Pete reached back inside the house and lifted out the three garbage bags. The scene looked weird as anything. Why would a boy be taking garbage bags out of a second-floor window?

Pete stepped over to the edge of the roof and, one by one, dropped the garbage bags down to the ground. Pete was about to climb into the tree, when, all of a sudden, the man turned toward the house!

Bennet nearly shrieked. He had to do something—and fast. He heaved the football high into the air. On its descent, the football crashed onto the hood of the green sedan with a loud *thwack!* The ball bounced off and took several hops across Bennet's front lawn before it came to a stop near the Ordways' front walkway.

"Hey!" shouted the man as he hopped out of the car. He leaned across the hood and rubbed his hand over the spot where the football had hit. He peered at Bennet with a menacing look. "You could've dented my car!" he said.

"Sorry!" said Bennet. Peering past the man, Bennet saw Pete jump down from the tree, pick up the garbage bags, and scurry behind his house.

"W-w-well, see ya!" Bennet said to the man. With that, he ran over, picked up his football, and, tucking it under his arm like a running back, dashed behind his house. Once out of the man's sight, Bennet dropped the football, hopped over the stone wall, and hurried into the woods. He met Pete by the tree that held the antenna.

"Nice work!" said Pete, patting Bennet on the back.

"I thought f-f-for sure he saw you," said Bennet, out of breath.

"You ever think about going out for football?" asked Pete.

"Very f-f-funny," said Bennet. He peered up at the antenna, which was cradled high above them in the branches. "C'mon, let's get the ant-t-tenna and get out of here."

Pete scampered up the tree, ripped the antenna from the branches, and hurled it down. Bennet jumped out of the way as the antenna crashed onto the ground, breaking apart. Bennet snapped the antenna into smaller pieces; he then bent the main rod over his knee. He stuffed the antenna pieces into the garbage bags. Pete climbed down from the tree and picked up the sledding saucer and flung it into the woods as if it were a gigantic Frisbee. It didn't go far: It banged into a tree.

Instead of returning to Bennet's house—where the man in the green sedan might see them—Bennet and Pete hiked through the woods and came out at High Street, about half a mile away. Walking quickly, they lugged the garbage bags over to the Grand Union shopping center. They dumped one bag in the garbage Dumpster behind the Grand Union, one in a garbage Dumpster behind the Burger King down the street, and the last bag in a garbage can behind an automobile repair shop.

Bennet was hoping that the man in the green sedan would be gone by the time they returned to his house, but he wasn't. He was still parked in the same spot. Bennet and Pete hid behind a forsythia bush that was on the side of Bennet's house and peeked out at the car.

"What do you say we get some eggs and toss 'em at his car?" suggested Pete.

"And g-g-get in more t-t-trouble than we're already in?" said Bennet. "No, thanks."

Suddenly, over in the direction of Pete's house, a dog began to bark. It was Gus. Pete had him locked in the cellar. "I better go let Gus out before his barking gives us away," said Pete. "I'll take him for a walk in the street."

"Are you c-c-crazy?" exclaimed Bennet, his eyes wide with alarm. "That guy will see you!"

Pete put his hand on Bennet's shoulder. "I'm just kidding," he said. He got up and, saying goodbye, stole across to his own property.

Bennet took one more look at the car, and then he, too, crawled out from behind the bush. He snuck around to his backyard. As he stepped inside the house, he heard his father call out from the kitchen, "Is that you, Bennet?"

"Y-y-yes," answered Bennet. He was surprised his father was home. At breakfast that morning, he said he wouldn't be home from work until around three in the afternoon.

"Please come into the kitchen," his father called. "Your mother and I would like a word with you."

Neither of his parents said hello to Bennet when he walked into the room. His father was over by the kitchen sink, leaning against the counter, his arms folded and his face unshaven. His mother was seated at the kitchen table, with a mug of tea in front of her, which she hadn't touched. They both looked very grim.

"Y-y-yes," said Bennet, stopping in the doorway.

"Come in here and sit down," said his mother.

Bennet took a seat at the kitchen table across from his mother. He could feel his heart banging inside his chest.

"I want you to look me straight in the eye and answer me yes or no," said his father. "Are you behind Deep Doo-doo?"

Bennet began to jiggle his legs. He didn't know what to say. He didn't want to lie, but he also didn't want to get in trouble. All of a sudden he thought of the Watergate break-in. Bennet could understand why President Nixon and his staff didn't tell the truth about their involvement in the Watergate burglary. For a brief moment, Bennet, too, considered lying about his involvement in Deep Doo-doo. But he knew *he* had to tell the truth. For one thing, lying would only get him into more trouble. For another, unlike the Watergate conspirators, he had to look his father straight in the eye and answer.

"Well?" said his mother.

Bennet glanced at his father and then lowered his gaze to the floor. "Y-y-yes," he said in a soft, barely audible voice.

His father groaned. His mother became furious. "Why in God's name did you ever do such a thing?" she demanded.

Bennet shrugged. "W-w-we w-w-were j-j-just t-t-trying to t-t-tell the t-t-truth about the g-g-governor," he said, his voice trembling. He glanced over at his father. Mr. Ordway was rubbing his eyes with the heels of his palms.

"Do you have any idea how much trouble

you're in?" said his mother. "You've broken broadcasting laws. The FBI is after you. You could go to jail." She began to cry.

"I-I-I d-d-didn't mean any harm," said Bennet.

"Who else helped you do this?" asked his mother, wiping her eyes.

"Who else?" said Bennet.

"Is Pete involved in this, too?"

"P-p-pete?"

"He is, isn't he?" said his mother. "How about Jimmy over at B & G's Hardware? Is he part of this?"

"No!" cried Bennet. "He d-d-doesn't know a thing ab-b-bout it."

"Are you telling us the truth?"

"Y-y-yes!" said Bennet. "Honest."

Just then, like a smoldering volcano, Mr. Ordway erupted. He slammed his fist down on the kitchen counter. Both Bennet and his mother jumped. "How could you do this?" he bellowed. "Do you know what you've done? My career may be ruined—all because of you! You've not only embarrassed your mother and me, but you've made a joke of the newspaper by sending me those notes. You've made a mockery of investigative journalism! People may even think I'm involved in this! My integrity is at stake! Didn't the consequences of what you were doing ever occur to you? You might go to jail! I might lose my job! All because of a dumb little stunt!" His father's face was burning with anger. He thrust his hand out and pointed toward the door. "Now get up to your room this instant!" he shouted. "Get up there before I *really* lose my temper!"

Bennet burst into tears. Sobbing, he ran out of the room.

After Bennet left the kitchen, Mr. Ordway made three phone calls. The first phone call was to his lawyer, since Bennet would be needing a lawyer when charges were brought against him. The second phone call was to the FBI agent who was handling the Deep Doo-doo investigation—the one who had questioned Mr. Ordway about Deep Doo-doo. The last phone call was to Trombly at his home.

"What's up, Ordway?" asked Trombly. "Did you hear from Deep Doo-doo again?"

"I know Deep Doo-doo's secret identity," said Mr. Ordway, on the verge of tears.

"You do?" cried Trombly excitedly on the other end. "Does he want to come forward?"

"Yes," said Mr. Ordway. "Yes, he does. But—" Mr. Ordway had to stop talking, he was so choked up.

"Yeah?" said Trombly impatiently. "Yeah, but what?"

"I-I can't cover the story."

Trombly snorted in disbelief. *"Why not?"*

Mr. Ordway tried to answer, but couldn't. He knew that if he spoke, he would only break into tears.

Best News I've Heard All Day!

Channel 2 was the first to break the story. At 3:48 on Saturday afternoon, during a nationally televised college football game, a special news bulletin crawled across the bottom of the screen, announcing that the police had made an arrest in the Deep Doo-doo case. In retrospect, it really was no surprise that Channel 2 was the first to report the story. For several days now they had stationed a reporter in front of the Ordways' house, just in case anything happened. He kept watch out on the street, in a green sedan.

Soon all the television stations were reporting the story. "There's been a surprising twist in the Deep Doo-doo story," announced an excited Channel 4 anchorwoman. Seated at the anchor desk, she reported the news with such enthusiasm you would have thought Channel 4 had broken the story. "Just moments ago, police arrested two twelve-year-old boys in connection with Deep Doo-doo! We have Susan Gargano standing by live outside police headquarters in North Agaming. So, Susan, can you tell us what's going on there?"

The TV screen cut to a woman in a khaki raincoat standing on the sidewalk outside police headquarters, with a noisy crowd of people behind her. Speaking into a hand-held microphone, she said, "Details are still sketchy at this point, Katy, but it appears as though two twelve-year-old boys were behind the whole Deep Doo-doo affair."

"What about the dog?" asked the anchorwoman, back at the station.

The TV reporter placed a hand to her ear, in which she was wearing a small earphone. "I'm sorry, I'm having trouble hearing you."

"The dog. Do we have any information on the dog?"

"Yes, we do," said the TV reporter. "According to police, Deep Doo-doo is a black Labrador retriever that belongs to one of the boys."

"How did they beam the dog onto people's TV sets?" asked the anchorwoman.

The reporter held her hand over her ear again. "I can't hear you, Katy," she said.

"How did they televise Deep Doo-doo?"

"Apparently, the boys built a high-powered television transmitter," said the TV reporter.

"Do police have this transmitter?"

"What was that?"

"Have police seized the transmitter?"

The TV reporter shook her head. "I'm sorry, Katy, I'm having trouble hearing—wait, this may be the police bringing in the boys."

Two police cars pulled up in front of the station. While police officers on the sidewalk held back the throng of reporters and spectators, several burly officers escorted Bennet and Pete up the steps to the station. Mr. and Mrs. Ordway and Mr. Ordway's lawyer walked beside Bennet. Mrs. Nickowsky walked beside Pete. Pete pulled his denim jacket up over his head to hide his face— just as he had seen people on TV do after they were arrested. At the end of the procession came Gus and a short, stocky policeman. The officer had Gus tied to a leash. Tail wagging, tongue hanging out, Gus veered from reporter to reporter. It was all the policeman could do to pull Gus along. As Bennet and Pete were led into the police station, reporters bombarded them with questions.

"What did you do with the transmitter?"

"How long did it take you to build it?"

"How long have you been planning this?"

"What happened to Sick and Tired?"

At one point, Bennet, against the prior advice of his father's lawyer, stopped and spoke to one TV reporter. "W-w-we d-d-didn't m-m-mean any h-h-harm," he said. Before he could say another word, Mr. Ordway's lawyer put his hand on Bennet's shoulder and led him through the doors of the police station, away from all the reporters.

• • •

Since it was the last weekend before the election, the governor was on the campaign trail when all this happened. He was upstate, speaking to a gathering of war veterans, so he had no idea that there'd been a break in the Deep Doo-doo case. It wasn't until he was walking away from the podium, waving and smiling to the applauding veterans, that a young TV reporter approached him and, holding a microphone in his face, said, "Governor, what do you think of the break in the Deep Doo-doo case?"

Surprised, the governor said, "There's been a break?"

"The police made an arrest just minutes ago," said the TV reporter. He stepped aside so that the cameraman could get a good shot of the governor's reaction.

The governor looked stunned. He hadn't expected news of this sort. Breaking into a big grin, he said, "Why, I'm delighted! I'm always glad when criminals are off the street." Then, as the news began to sink in, he added, cheerfully, "Best news I've heard all day!"

The governor was overjoyed to hear that there'd been an arrest in the Deep Doo-doo case. It meant he could go on TV again without fear of being interrupted by Deep Doo-doo. He was overjoyed, that is, until he found out that the culprits behind Deep Doo-doo were two twelve-year-old boys. He was even more dismayed when, a little later, he viewed a tape of Bennet and Pete being led away by the police. He watched in silence while Bennet said, "W-w-we d-d-didn't m-m-mean any h-h-harm." The governor threw up his hands and groaned. "Oh, that's just great!" he said. "Not only is it two young boys, but one boy stutters!"

Having been in politics nearly all his adult life, the governor was no stranger to the power of public opinion. He knew that people watching on TV would feel sorry for these two boys—especially the boy with the stutter. People would immediately side with the boys over the governor. They would see the boys under arrest, and then they would see the governor's reaction. "Best news I've heard all day!" they'd hear him say. The worst part was, the TV stations would run the clip over and over again, so if you happened to miss it the first time it was shown, you were sure to see it on a later newscast. "Best news I've heard all day! Best news I've heard all day!" Everyone would think that the governor was delighted by these two families' misfortunes.

Within an hour after the arrest, a small but vocal band of demonstrators gathered outside the police station. "Free the Deep Doo-doo Two! Free the Deep Doo-doo Two!" they chanted over and over, louder and louder.

As darkness set in, the crowd, rather than dwindling, grew. And grew. And grew. Soon there were a hundred demonstrators. Then two hundred. Then five hundred. They vowed not to leave until all charges against the Deep Doo-doo Two—as they referred to Bennet and Pete—were dropped.

The TV networks gave extensive coverage to the demonstration. The governor, who had canceled the rest of that day's campaign rallies to keep on top of the story, watched the events unfold on TV. No political advisor had to tell him how damaging this was to his reelection bid. Nobody had to tell him this was not the kind of news coverage he needed—particularly three days before the election.

Some Welcome Home

After Bennet was placed under arrest, he just sobbed and sobbed. He was so frightened. He thought the police would be angry at him for all the trouble he and Pete had caused. But, strangely enough, they weren't. In fact, they were actually quite friendly to him—even going so far as to congratulate him.

"Nice work, kid," said the young policewoman who read the charges against him.

"Thanks for telling it like it is," said another police officer, who then asked Bennet for his autograph.

"So what kind of radio tubes did you use?" asked the FBI agent who questioned Bennet at the police station. He seemed amazed—awed even— that two twelve-year-old boys were able to build such a sophisticated transmitting device.

As for Pete, he wasn't a bit upset about being under arrest. On the contrary, he was having the time of his life. To Pete, the whole thing was still a wonderful adventure. After he was read his rights, Pete insisted on being handcuffed, even though the police officer who arrested him said that, for this type of a crime, handcuffs weren't necessary. But Pete made such a fuss that the police officer finally obliged. The moment the handcuffs were snapped on his wrists, Pete tried to squirm out of them as if he were Harry Houdini. When Pete was released in his mother's custody, he begged the police officer to leave the handcuffs on for just a little longer— he was about to slip out of them any second, he really was, he said. Once reunited with Gus, Pete had Gus perform tricks for a group of police officers. They laughed and clapped at each trick.

After Bennet was released in his parents' custody, he and his parents got into their car and drove home. Mr. Ordway, who drove, didn't say a word. He was still fuming about Deep Doo-doo. He also had the worst headache. He just wanted to go home, lie down on the living room couch, close his eyes, and try to forget the whole incident had ever happened. But alas, when he turned down his street, he saw a large crowd of reporters assembled in front of his house.

"Oh, no!" groaned Mr. Ordway.

"What are *they* doing here?" asked Mrs. Ordway.

"I imagine they want to interview Bennet," said Mr. Ordway. He heaved a deep sigh. "Some welcome home!"

"Look at all those cameras!" cried Mrs. Ordway in astonishment. In the backseat, Bennet gaped at the cameras, which sat on tripods upon their front lawn, aimed directly at the house.

Two reporters stood in the Ordways' driveway. They had to leap out of the way when Mr. Ordway, braking, swung the car into his driveway. As he pulled up to the garage, reporters ran alongside the car.

"Walk straight into the house," Mr. Ordway instructed his family. "Don't say a word to anyone."

Like bees around honey, the reporters swarmed around the Ordways when they emerged from their car. The Ordways marched into the house without answering a single question. Closing the front door behind him, Mr. Ordway turned to Bennet and told him to go up to his bedroom and stay there until he was told he could come down. "And under no circumstances are you to open your window and talk to any of the reporters on the street," said Mr. Ordway.

On Sunday, the reporters were still there. They seemed to have multiplied during the night. The Ordways didn't leave their house. They didn't even go to church. Curiously, Mr. Ordway found he hated being on the other side of the camera lens— that is, being the focus of the news rather than reporting it. He hated being trapped inside his house, particularly on such a beautiful, sunny Indian summer day. It was a perfect day to toss a football around in the backyard with your son. Not that Mr. Ordway ever did such things. Bennet wasn't much of a football player. Looking for something to do, Mr. Ordway turned on the TV to watch a pro football game. But it was halftime. The halftime show had been preempted—by a special report about Deep Doo-doo. A reporter had interviewed some of the people who knew Bennet and Pete.

"They seemed like such nice students," said Ms. Brinkley, their elderly social studies teacher, speaking in front of the school. "Who would ever have thought."

"I can't believe it was Bennet and Pete," said Paula Lebowitz, a classmate.

"Hey, give them a break," said Jimmy Petrie of B & G's Hardware. He was standing behind the counter of his hardware store. "They're just kids."

The station cut to a commercial for an extra-strength pain reliever. The camera technique used in the commercial had been inspired by Deep Doo-

doo's broadcasts—it had that identical shaky camera look to it.

Groaning, Mr. Ordway turned off the TV.

Bennet's Sunday was even worse. He had to spend the entire day up in his room. He wasn't even allowed to speak on the phone. At one point, Jimmy called him. Pressing his ear to his bedroom door, Bennet heard his mother talking to Jimmy on the phone. From what Bennet could make out, it sounded as though Jimmy was calling to see how he was.

Sometime toward the end of the afternoon, Bennet looked out his window. Over on Pete's front lawn, he saw Pete giving an interview to the reporters. Pete abruptly turned and pointed to Bennet's window. The reporters all turned and peered up at the window. The news photographers raised their cameras. Bennet waved to them and the photographers clicked away. The photograph appeared on the front page of many of the next day's newspapers. It showed Bennet, looking terribly forlorn, waving from his bedroom window, a captive in his own house.

Tom Ordway's Article

On Monday morning, the day before the election, it was decided that Bennet should stay home from school so he wouldn't be hounded by reporters. Mrs. Ordway also stayed home to make sure none of the reporters got any bright ideas and tried to venture into the house to obtain an exclusive interview with Bennet. Only Mr. Ordway left the house that day. He got up very early, while it was still dark, and went in to work. He had to get out of the house. If he had to spend one more day cooped up inside the house, he would have gone crazy.

When Mr. Ordway arrived at work, he found a note from Trombly on his desk asking him to come by his office. He was surprised to find the note, as Trombly never got in this early in the morning. Mr. Ordway set his briefcase on his desk and took off his coat. As he crossed the quiet newsroom to Trombly's office, he felt a sickening sensation in his stomach. He was convinced that Trombly was angry at him because Deep Doo-doo had turned out to be Bennet. By writing about Deep Doo-doo without even realizing it was his own son, Mr. Ordway had embarrassed the newspaper. "I guess this is it," Mr. Ordway said to himself. "I'm going to be fired."

Trombly was at his desk, talking on the phone. "Yes, I agree," he said as, looking up, he saw Mr. Ordway. He waved him into his office. "I agree with you: Something has to be done. Well, he just walked into my office. Yes, I'll handle it." Trombly hung up the phone. He looked at Mr. Ordway and said, "Sit down, Tom."

Mr. Ordway sat down.

"Guess who that was."

"Stevenson?" asked Mr. Ordway as he nervously jiggled his legs.

Trombly nodded. "Tom," he said, folding his hands and looking very earnestly at Mr. Ordway, "you know this Deep Doo-doo incident has made us look pretty silly."

Mr. Ordway said, "I know it has. And I'm sorry."

"What are you sorry about?"

"Well, it was my kid and—"

Trombly scowled. He waved his hand at him, saying, "We all fell for it. These things happen."

He hesitated a moment before adding, "But we will have to do something about it, you understand."

Mr. Ordway gazed down at his shoes. He had a huge lump in his throat. "Are you going to fire me?"

Trombly made a face. "Good lord, no! You're one of my best reporters."

Mr. Ordway closed his eyes in relief. He sighed. A great weight had been lifted from his chest.

"It simply means that I'm taking you off the Deep Doo-doo story," said Trombly. "Whether you like it or not, you, too, are now involved in this whole Deep Doo-doo mess. In other words, your reporting won't be objective."

"I understand," said Mr. Ordway. "Frankly, I'm just as glad to be off the story."

"I do have another assignment for you, however," said Trombly. "It's an article, one only Tom Ordway could write."

Mr. Ordway smiled. "What's that?"

"I'd like you to try your hand at writing a personal article," said Trombly.

Mr. Ordway looked perplexed. "A personal article?"

"Yes," said Trombly. "I thought you could write an article from your point of view on what happened over the weekend in regard to Deep Doo-doo. You know, a real emotional article. Tell how you found out it was Bennet. How you felt after you found out. How you feel now. Things like that."

Mr. Ordway held up his hands, palms out. "Thank you," he said. "But I don't think I'm really up to writing this article."

Trombly looked Mr. Ordway in the eye and said, "I'm afraid you don't understand, Tom. I'm not suggesting you write this article. I'm telling you to."

Mr. Ordway stood. "I'll get started on it right this minute."

"Oh, and Tom," said Trombly as Mr. Ordway was about to leave his office. Mr. Ordway turned and looked at him. "I want you to title your article 'Family Values.'"

Back in his office, Mr. Ordway sat in front of his computer and tried to write his article. He couldn't think of anything to say. His mind was a total blank. While he had written many articles about other people, he had never actually written one about himself. He couldn't understand why Trombly wanted him to title the article "Family Values." What did he, Bennet, and Deep-doo Doo have to do with family values? It didn't make sense. But then, nothing made sense to him anymore. Just a few days ago, he had been a big hero, the only reporter Deep Doo-doo was leaving notes for. And now everyone had all but forgotten him. Now his son and his son's best friend were the big heroes. Mr. Ordway still couldn't believe Bennet knew how to build such a complicated thing as a transmitter. Obviously, he didn't know his son very well. Maybe if he had, he wouldn't have been so surprised to find out that Bennet was behind Deep Doo-doo. Maybe if he knew his son better, none of this would ever have happened in the first place. Just then, Mr. Ordway had a flash of inspiration. Suddenly he knew what to write his article about. Typing on his keyboard, his fingers raced to keep up with his thoughts. The article pretty much wrote itself, in fact.

About an hour later, as he was reading over what he had written, making sure it read okay and that there were no misspelled words, the phone rang. It was Mrs. Ordway.

"Tom!" she said excitedly, in a breathless voice. "I think you'd better come home!"

"Why?" asked Mr. Ordway, alarmed. "What's the matter?"

"Nothing. Everything is fine."

"What is it then?"

"Well," said Mrs. Ordway on the other end. "We have a visitor."

The Visitor

When Bennet awoke that Monday morning, he did what he usually did on a school-day morning. He showered, dressed, stuffed what books he was taking with him to school into his backpack, put on his Boston Red Sox cap, and came downstairs for breakfast. It was then that his mother told him he would not be going to school. The two of them, she said, were staying home that day—only he had to spend the day in his room.

Bennet thought he would cry. He hated being stuck in his room. It was so incredibly boring. At eight o'clock, the time school started, Bennet imagined himself at school, filing into homeroom. At ten minutes past eight, he saw himself seated in his first class, science. The more he thought about school, the more he missed it. He missed his teachers. He missed the other kids. He missed Pete. He even missed the crummy cafeteria food and gym class. He wondered if he would ever be allowed to go back to school again. He hoped he wouldn't be sent off to reform school.

. . .

To try to keep his mind off such thoughts, Bennet opened his notebook and began to design a remote-control vacuum cleaner that he hoped to build one day. He was trying to figure out how he would wire the thing when he heard a lot of commotion outside the house. Bennet got up from his desk, went to his window, and looked out. A police car and a long black limousine had pulled up to his house. Who could this be? Bennet asked himself. Whoever it was was sure making the reporters excited. With a loud clamor, they pushed to get as close as possible to the limousine. They paid no attention to the lone policeman who was stationed in front of the Ordways' house, trying to hold them back.

The back door of the limousine swung open and several people climbed out, including a tall man in glasses wearing a dark suit. The tall man waved to the reporters as he and his entourage walked across the Ordways' front lawn toward the house. The tall man gazed up at Bennet's window. Bennet's heart nearly did a back flip when he saw the man's face.

It was the governor!

• • •

After Mr. Ordway got off the phone with his wife, he rushed right home. Turning down his street, he saw the black limousine parked in front of his house. With a spin of the steering wheel, he pulled the car into his driveway. The moment he stepped out of the car, he was surrounded by reporters. Mr. Ordway didn't answer a single one of their questions. He hurried into the house, where he met his wife in the kitchen. She was pouring hot coffee into her best china cups. "Where is he?" asked Mr. Ordway.

Mrs. Ordway bit her bottom lip and pointed to the living room. Mr. Ordway peeked into the living room. The governor was seated, legs crossed, on the couch. He was looking curiously about the room while two of his aides huddled together in the middle of the room and several security men stood nearby, keeping a watchful eye on things. Mr. Ordway stepped back into the kitchen. "Did he say what he wants?" he whispered to his wife.

Mrs. Ordway shook her head. "The only thing he's said is that he has something to talk to us about," she replied. "We've been waiting for you to come home."

Mr. Ordway straightened his necktie and

marched into the living room. "Governor," he said.

The governor sprang up from the couch. He held out his hand, smiling. "It's Tom, isn't it?" he said as the two men shook hands.

"What brings you here?" asked Mr. Ordway.

"Well, I thought we might talk," said the governor and then added "Tom," as though he were a good friend of Mr. Ordway's.

Mr. Ordway gestured for the governor to sit down. "What would you like to talk about?" he asked.

"Well," said the governor, taking a seat on the couch, "I thought we might include the whole family in on this—including your son, Bennet."

Mr. Ordway gave a quick glance at Mrs. Ordway, who had just brought in the tray of coffee. "I'll get him," said Mr. Ordway. He rose and went out to the front hallway. He stood at the foot of the stairs that led up to the second floor and shouted, "Bennet, could you come down here for a minute."

Up in his bedroom, Bennet was nervously pacing the floor. He didn't know *what* was going on. He couldn't believe the governor was in his house. *The governor!* Heart pounding, he opened his bedroom door and came down the stairs. He was terrified of meeting the governor. After saying all those horrible things about him, who wouldn't be? But if the governor was angry at Bennet, he certainly didn't show it. Indeed, he broke into a big grin when Bennet appeared in the doorway. This made Bennet even more nervous.

"Hello, Bennet!" said the governor cheerfully, setting down his cup. He stood and shook Bennet's hand.

"H-h-hello," said Bennet.

"Please, son, have a seat," said the governor as if it were the governor's house. He turned to one of his aides and nodded. The aides and security men left the room, leaving the governor alone with Mr. and Mrs. Ordway and Bennet.

"I thought you might like to know what's transpired in the past twenty-four hours," said the governor. "I've been doing quite a bit of behind-the-scenes maneuvering, and I'm happy to say that I've managed to have all charges dropped against Bennet and his friend, Pete."

Mrs. Ordway let out a gasp and cried, "That's great!"

Bennet was stunned. "Th-thanks!" he said.

Mr. Ordway, smiling, said, "We all thank you."

The governor smiled broadly. Then, crossing his legs, he continued, "Now I was wondering if you might like to do me a small favor."

Mr. Ordway eyed the governor suspiciously. "What kind of favor?"

The governor laughed. "Oh, nothing much," he said. "I was hoping you might like to endorse me, that's all."

"Endorse you?" said Mr. Ordway, with a glance at Mrs. Ordway.

"Yes," said the governor, turning very serious. "I'm asking for your endorsement."

"That would probably help you in the election, wouldn't it?" said Mr. Ordway.

The smile returned to the governor's face. "It couldn't hurt."

"Have you asked Pete's family for their endorsement?" asked Mrs. Ordway.

The governor said, "Well, no."

"Probably just as well," said Mr. Ordway. "Pete's parents are divorced. They're not the sort of family you want endorsing you—a man who believes in strong family values."

"You know, Tom, I've been reading a lot of your articles lately," said the governor. "You're a fine writer. In fact, I think you'd make a darn good press secretary."

"What's a p-p-press secretary?" asked Bennet.

"A press secretary is an elected official's spokesperson to the press," said Mr. Ordway.

"A press secretary also makes a lot more money than most reporters," added the governor.

"I'm sure that's true," said Mr. Ordway.

"The more I think about it, the more I think you'd make one fantastic press secretary, Tom," said the governor. "How about it? Will you endorse me? And then come onboard?"

Bennet, Mrs. Ordway, and the governor all fixed their curious eyes on Mr. Ordway. The room was dead silent. This was one of the most important moments in Mr. Ordway's life, and they all knew it, even Bennet. Finally, Mr. Ordway, blinking, gave a little cough, and said, "You know, Governor, if you've been reading my articles, you may be interested in reading what I've written for tomorrow's paper. It's all about family values."

"Is it?" said the governor. He looked more uncomfortable than interested.

"Yes," said Mr. Ordway. "Actually, it's about this family right here in this room. You see, I learned something from my son these past few days."

Bennet, surprised, stared at his father.

"My son stood up for what he believed was the

right thing to do, and he said it. While the way he did it may not have been quite legal, it is kind of amazing when you think about it, that two twelve-year-old boys could pull off such a thing. Don't you think?"

"I suppose," said the governor.

"I don't think anyone was more surprised than I was to find out that my son was Deep Doo-doo. You know what all this has taught me, Governor? This has taught me that I really don't know my son very well. But I intend to correct that." Lifting his cup, he took a sip of coffee. "I've learned something else. Bennet has showed me that you have to stand up for what you believe in."

The governor looked as though he didn't quite understand. "Which means what?" he asked.

"Which means I cannot and I will not endorse you," said Mr. Ordway. He stood. "Now if you'll excuse me, I have to get back to work." He paused as though he suddenly remembered something. He looked over at Bennet. "Oh, Bennet," he said. "If it's okay with your mom, you're free to leave your room."

Bennet could scarcely believe what he had just witnessed. "Th-th-thanks!" he said happily.

The governor raced after Mr. Ordway as he headed for the door. "Okay, fine," the governor said. "I understand why you don't want to endorse me. But how about a picture together with the whole family as I announce the news that all charges are being dropped against Bennet and Pete?"

Mr. Ordway just shook his head and said, "Sorry, no can do."

The Election

The next day, Election Day, it rained. Despite the dreary weather, voter turnout was extremely heavy. The polls opened at seven, and exit polls conducted throughout the day showed the governor and his challenger running neck and neck. Clearly, the governor had been helped by his announcement the day before that all charges against Bennet and Pete were being dropped. At three o'clock, the gray clouds that had covered most of the southern half of the state blew away as a cold front passed through. The sun appeared, shining brightly. Curiously enough, the reporters who had been camped out in front of the Ordways' house had also disappeared. It was as though they had been blown away with the clouds. Now that Deep Doo-doo was no longer an important news story, they had gone off to cover other stories.

The polls closed at nine o'clock sharp. Within

minutes after closing, all the TV networks projected the governor's challenger the winner. By ten o'clock, with over half the precincts in, the governor, trailing by over ten percentage points, conceded the race.

Unavailable for Comment

The morning after the election, a reporter called on the Ordways in the hope of speaking to Bennet and getting his comments on the election. He didn't get very far, though. He was met at the door by Mrs. Ordway, who refused to let him in.

"Bennet is unavailable for comment," she said.

"What's he doing today?" asked the reporter, who apparently knew he wasn't in school.

"He's unavailable" was all Mrs. Ordway would say.

"Well, then, may I speak to Tom Ordway about the election?" asked the reporter. Apparently, he had also tried to call Mr. Ordway at work and found that he had taken the day off.

"I'm afraid he's unavailable at the moment, too," said Mrs. Ordway.

"I don't suppose you have anything to say?"

"Sorry," said Mrs. Ordway, and shut the door.

Mrs. Ordway entered the kitchen. The breakfast

dishes were still on the table. She stepped over to the kitchen sink and pulled on a pair of pink latex dish-washing gloves. Clearing off the table, she rinsed the dishes off and stacked them in the dishwasher. She was about to dump what was left of the coffee into the sink when she thought she'd just check and make sure Mr. Ordway didn't want another cup. She walked out to the front hallway and opened the door that led down to the cellar. The cellar light was on.

"So what's this do?" she heard Mr. Ordway ask.

"This th-thing?" said Bennet's voice excitedly. "This is an electric shoe lacer."

"A *what*?"

"An electric shoe lacer."

"You built *this*?"

"P-p-pete and I did," said Bennet. "G-go ahead, turn it on."

There was a loud, pulsating electric hum.

"This is terrific!" shouted Mr. Ordway, laughing over the noise.

"It has three speeds, too."

The noise stopped. "So," said Mr. Ordway. "What are we going to work on?"

"A remote-control vacuum c-c-cleaner."

"A remote-control vacuum cleaner!"

"It's Mom's Christmas p-present."

"Think it'll really work?"

"Why w-wouldn't it?"

Mr. Ordway laughed. "Silly question," he said. "Let's get started."

Mrs. Ordway decided not to interrupt them, after all. She quietly closed the door and returned to the kitchen. Pouring the rest of the coffee into the sink, she laughed to herself as she thought about the remote-control vacuum cleaner. What on earth would she possibly do with a remote-control vacuum cleaner, she wondered.

But if Mr. Ordway also thought a remote-control vacuum cleaner was a weird idea, he never said so. Using parts bought only at B & G's Hardware, he and Bennet spent many nights and weekends together building the contraption. Pete helped a little, but not that much. He was too busy. After hearing that the governor—the *ex*-governor, that is—was writing his memoirs, which were sure to include the Deep Doo-doo affair, Pete got busy writing his own memoirs about Deep Doo-doo. He knew he couldn't trust the governor to tell the true story about how two boys and a dog caused—as one newspaper article put it during the very height of the Deep Doo-doo hysteria—the biggest political furor in the state's history. No, only he or Bennet could write *that* story. And since Bennet was all wrapped up building a remote-control vacuum cleaner with his father, that left only himself.

Pete opened his spiral-bound notebook, sharpened his pencil, and began to write.

Michael Delaney is a freelance writer and the author of several books for young readers. He lives in Greenwich, Connecticut.

TRIVIA
MADNESS

1000 Fun Trivia Questions
About Anything

**Trivia Quiz Questions
and Answers
Vol 3**

By
Bill O'Neill

ISBN-13: 978-1537495521

DISCLAIMER

This book contain trivia questions and answers and
funny facts that will make any quiz challenge
enjoyable. I hope you like movie trivia and music
trivia because this book has it, a thousand of them!
Enjoy the quizzes!

What city's homeless canines have learned to ride the local subways for commuting between locations?

Moscow

, .

What was so special about Clay Henry III of Lajitas, TX?

He was a beer drinking goat, elected the town's mayor in 1986

, .

What is the only letter of the alphabet that does not appear in any U.S. state or territory name?

The letter "Q"

, .

Who was put into witness protection in Lake Charles, Louisiana after testifying against their owner?

A parrot named Echo

, .

What is the only month that can pass without a full moon?

February

, ·

What was the first product with a UPC scanner bar code?

Wrigley gum

, ·

What movie scene took three days to film, and used nearly 60 doors?

"Here's Johnny!" from "The Shining"

, ·

Particles of what metal can be found inside human hair?

Gold

, ·

Depending on wind speed, what can travel up to 100 miles per hour across the sky?

Clouds

, ·

Who is awarded the most posthumous Vietnam War Medal of Honor awards?

Those soldiers who covered enemy grenades to protect their comrades.

, .

In a standard deck of cards, which is the only king without a mustache?

King of Hearts

, .

What can release more energy that all the world's nuclear weapons?

Hurricanes

, .

Which book is the most widely stolen from public libraries?

Guinness Book of Records

, .

Where do black bears hibernate, sometimes?

In tops of trees

, .

What professional sport began in Hoboken, New Jersey in 1849?

Baseball

, .

How is electric power generated on the island country of Tokelau?

100 percent solar power

, .

What is the most popular gift for Dad on Father's Day?

Neckties

, .

Which country sells more board games than any other?

Germany

, .

For one day (September 27, 1777), which city was the United States capital?

Lancaster, Pennsylvania

, .

For each human on Earth, there are 1.6 million of what insect?

Ants

, .

In 1974, where did John Lennon sign the contract that disbanded the Beatles?

Walt Disney World

, .

Shortly after its release, two California men fell off a cliff while playing what virtual reality game?

Pokemon Go

, .

What country opened the world's highest and longest glass bottom bridge in 2016?

China

, .

Popular during the days of the Old West, the Pony Express mail service operated for how long?

19 months

, .

Created in 1958, what was the first video game called?

Tennis for Two

✦ ·

Who was Time Magazine's 'Man of the Year' of 1938?

Adolph Hitler

✦ ·

What string instrument is assembled with 70 separate pieces of wood?

Violin

✦ ·

What cannot fly if their body temperature reaches less than 86 degrees?

Butterflies

✦ ·

During early pregnancy, how fast do neurons multiply?

250,000 neurons per minute

✦ ·

What city recently built a fitness playground for senior citizens?

Barcelona, Spain

ɾ ·

What is the deadliest job in America, statistically?

President

ɾ ·

What country did one man try to sell on eBay in 2006?

New Zealand

ɾ ·

5.7 million Americans suffer from what condition?

Heart failure

ɾ ·

What did Durex name their Ramses condom after?

Ramses II, who fathered over 160 children

ɾ ·

What are the names of the three wise monkeys?

Mizaru (See no evil), Mikazaru (Hear no evil), and Mazaru (Speak no evil)

, .

What does McDonald's classify its frequent customers as?

Heavy users

, .

What does the average person spend six months of their lifetime doing?

Waiting for a red light to turn green

, .

Humans burn more calories when sleeping, rather than what?

Watching television

, .

What was Al Capone's profession, according to his business card?

Used furniture dealer

, .

How long is the Statue of Liberty's index finger?

Eight feet long

, .

What warehouse is so big it contains its own rainclouds?

NASA Vehicle Assembly Building

, .

What city banned outdoor advertising, removing over 300,000 signs and billboards?

Sao Paulo, Brazil

, .

What does the ZIP in ZIP Code stand for?

Zone Improvement Plan

, .

A ball of what material will bounce higher than a rubber ball?

Glass

, .

Jimi Hendrix, Janis Joplin, and Jim Morrison were each how old when they died?

27 years' old

, .

Who was the inspiration for the bully Biff Tannen in "Back to the Future"?

Donald Trump

, .

Alligators, dragon lizards, ferrets, gerbils, geckos, hamsters, monk parakeets, piranhas, snakes, snapping turtles, and toucans are prohibited to own as a pet in what state?

Hawaii

, .

Where was the dice game Yahtzee created?

Aboard a yacht

, .

Where was the time zone first adopted?

New Zealand

, .

Ground beef, poultry, pork, and seafood can be stored in the refrigerator for how long?

3 to 5 days

, •

A watermelon contains how much water?

92 percent water

, •

How fast is the speed of light?

186,282 miles per second

, •

How many championships has Richard Petty won?

Richard Petty and Dale Earnhardt Sr. both have won seven championships

, •

What is the German word for excess weight due to overeating?

Kummerspeck

, •

A study found that 80 percent of all fatal car crashes are caused by what?

Male drivers

، .

How much saliva is produced by the average person in their lifetime?

Enough to fill two swimming pools

، .

What is hedonophobia?

The fear of feeling pleasure

، .

Who was the only person to have served as president and vice-president of the United States without being elected to the office?

Gerald Ford

، .

What was the animated series "The Powerpuff Girls" originally known as?

The WhoopAss Girls

، .

How many years of world peace has there been in the last 3,500 years?

230 years of peace

, .

What woman dressed as a man to join the Continental Army during the American Revolutionary War?

Deborah Sampson

, .

Sir Isaac Newton was known for his theory of gravity after seeing what fall from a tree?

An apple

, .

How did major league baseball pitcher Joel Zumaya miss three games in 2006?

He was injured playing Guitar Hero

, .

Who was the only U.S. president to go into battle while serving as president?

George Washington

, .

What holiday song was originally written in 1857 for a Thanksgiving celebration?

Jingle Bells

˒˙

What singer/actress poured candle wax on Willem Dafoe's chest in the movie "Body of Evidence"?

Madonna

ˌ ˙

What author was a failed KGB spy named Argo?

Ernest Hemingway

ˌ ˙

The real name of Shaggy from "Scooby-Doo" is what?

Norville Rogers

ˌ ˙

What children's toy was invented by architect Frank Lloyd Wright's son?

Lincoln Logs

ˌ ˙

Denmark, Norway, and Sweden are countries
that make up what region?

Scandinavia

, .

Temperature inversion causes what type of
precipitation?

Freezing rain

, .

According to knot theory, what is the simplest
way to tie a knot?

A simple loop

, .

What material was the first computer mouse
made of?

Wood

, .

What did the first ever text message say?

Merry Christmas

, .

Under extreme pressure, diamonds can be made from what?

Peanut Butter

, .

What has killed more humans than all wars combined?

Mosquitoes

, .

Who was the world's youngest billionaire?

Snapchat's founder Evan Spiegel

, .

What was film critic Leonard Maltin's review of the 1948 movie "Isn't it Romantic?"

"No."

, .

The content of what 1994 book by Michael Pearl has been linked to several child deaths?

To Train Up a Child

, .

What survived the 2003 Space Shuttle Columbia disaster?

Parasitic worms called nematodes

, .

Can some cats grow opposable thumbs?

Yes, they are called polydactyl cats, and the condition can occur in any cat population

, .

What is the sneeze reflex called?

Autosomal Dominant Compelling Helio-Ophthalmic Outburst Syndrome (ACHOO)

, .

To keep him safe, what does Nintendo forbid Nintendo legend Shigeru Miyamoto from doing?

They insist he does not walk or bike to work

, .

Doune Castle, used in the filming of the 1975 comedy "Monty Python and the Holy Grail" was also featured in what series?

Game of Thrones

, .

What beverage can reverse liver damage caused by alcohol?

Coffee

, .

What injuries are involved in a fourth degree burn?

Muscle or bone

, .

What video game features characters based on real historical figures, whose location and time of death are accurate?

Assassin's Creed

, .

In sound editor lingo, what does the name "R2-D2" stand for?

Reel Two, Dialog Two

, .

What is located at the temple where Julius Caesar was murdered?

A cat sanctuary

, .

Cashew nuts grow individually on what type of tree?

Cashew apple trees

, .

What Latin term did the word "muscle" come from?

Musculus, which means little mouse, because the flexed muscle looked like a mouse.

, .

What author was the first to use insults about people's mothers?

William Shakespeare

, .

What American newspaper was German socialist a European correspondent for?

New York Tribune

, .

What is described as doing something without emotional distress or reason?

Irrationality

, .

What forms of intimacy are proven to reduce stress instantly?

Hugging and holding hands

, .

What is egg white also known as?

Albumen

, .

Though less than 5 % of the world's population lives in the United States, they consume almost 37 % of what?

Cocaine

, .

What did a conman try to sell for scrap metal in 1925?

The Eiffel Tower

, .

The first fax machine was invented over 25 years before what?

The telephone

, .

Why do most pool tables have a green felt cover?

Billiards was once an outdoor lawn game

, .

What country was first to reach the moon's surface?

The Soviet Union's Luna 2 mission

, .

How many of the bones in your body are in your feet?

25% of all the bones in your body are in your feet

, .

How many eyes does a bee have?

A bee has five eyes, three simple eyes, and two compound eyes

, .

Can a cat move its lower jaw sideways?

A cat cannot move its lower jaw sideways, so it cannot chew large chunks of food.

, .

Why can't a crocodile stick out its tongue?

Because their tongue is attached to the roof of their mouth by a membrane.

, •

Why do birds bob their heads while they walk?

They bob their heads for depth perception

, •

If a male kangaroo is called a buck or a "boomer", what is a female kangaroo known as?

A doe or a "flyer"

, •

How fast can a honeybee fly?

A honeybee can reach a speed of about 20 miles per hour

, •

No matter how much random trivia you learn, how much does the brain weigh?

A human brain weighs about three pounds

, •

If a land mile is 5,280 feet, how long is one nautical mile?

One nautical mile is about 6,080 feet

, ·

What form of intimacy can burn 26 calories?

Kissing for one minute

, ·

When are the best times to see a rainbow?

In the morning or late afternoon

, ·

With about 4,000 beans on a coffee tree, how many coffee beans would make one cup?

100 coffee beans per cup

, ·

How fast is a sneeze?

A sneeze launches mucus from your body at about 100 miles per hr.

, ·

How much water does a 10 Gallon hat hold?

About three quarts of water

, •

What is the world's largest lake, by surface area?

Lake Superior

, •

United States has about how many pizzerias?

There are over 61,000 pizzerias in the U.S.

, •

How big was the first video cassette recorder?

The first VCR was introduced in 1956, and was about the size of a piano

, •

According to Guinness World Records, how much did the largest cheesecake weigh?

Created by Philadelphia Cream Cheese, it weighed 6,900 lbs.

, •

What was the first commercially successful bicycle nicknamed?

Hobby-horse

, •

Why does your tongue heal so fast?

The tongue heals faster because it contains so many blood vessels

’ ·

Which year can be read the same upside-down, and right-side up?

1961, the next year this will be possible will be 6009.

’ ·

When did the first televised soap-opera debut?

Faraway Hill debuted in 1946

’ ·

How many languages are spoken in the world?

Over 6,000 languages are spoken in the world today, many are only used by a few hundred people.

’ ·

What do Spain and Latin American countries traditionally do at midnight of December 31?

They eat 12 grapes with each bell strike to ward off evil

’ ·

What popular coconut based drink was created by a bartender in Puerto Rico?

Pina Colada

, .

Compared to other countries, how much does the U.S. spend on military expenditures annually?

United States spends more on military than the next seven countries combined.

, .

What member of the U.S. Navy during World War II wrote the article titled "Why I Hate My Uncle"?

Adolph Hitler's nephew, William Patrick Hitler

, .

What is the only show on U.S. television that has never used a theme song?

60 Minutes

, .

What 11th century work of classic Japanese literature is regarded as the world's first novel?

The Tale of Genji by Murasaki Shikibu

, .

How many abortions occur in the U.S. each year?

1.2 million women have an abortion every year

, .

How many people were rescued from the terrorist attacks of the World Trade Center on September 11, 2001?

18 people were rescued from the rubble

, .

How much oxygen is produced by the Amazon rainforest?

20% of the Earth's oxygen

, .

How long is summer on the planet Uranus?

Summer on Uranus lasts 42 years

, .

What did Japanese researchers develop to force people to stop speaking?

A gun

, .

Where do most earthquakes occur?

About 90% of the world's earthquakes occur along the "ring of fire" around the Pacific Ocean.

, .

How big is Walt Disney World Resort in Florida?

At nearly 40 square miles, it is almost the size of San Francisco.

, .

Did George Washington really chop down a cherry tree?

Author Parson Weems created the myth in his 1800 biography "The Life of Washington".

, .

What U.S. state is the world's fifth largest supplier of food?

California

, .

What is the number one suicide site in the entire world?

Golden Gate Bridge

, .

Did Alexander the Great ever lose a battle?

In his 15 years of conquest, he never lost a single battle.

, .

What is the second most populous island in Europe after Great Britain?

Ireland

, .

Why is South Africa called the "Rainbow Nation"?

It has 11 official languages

, .

What was the first South American city to get an electricity supply?

La Paz, Bolivia. It was originally powered by llama dung.

, .

Who was the youngest person to ever win the
Nobel Peace Prize?

Martin Luther King Jr.

, .

The F-word is used 265 times in what movie?

Pulp Fiction

, .

In 5,000 years of medical history, what is the
only disease to be eradicated?

Smallpox

, .

What can you legally do in the state of Florida
to save pets from overheating?

Smash the car window

, .

What did researchers at the Bristol Robotics
Laboratory discover can charge a cell phone?

Urine

, .

When compared in size, orbit, and composition, what planet is closest to Earth?

Venus

, .

How far must a bowling pin tilt in order to fall down?

A bowling pin only needs to tilt 7.5 degrees to fall down

, .

What outdoor recreation game was banned in Canada in 1989?

Lawn Darts

, .

Where is this strange warning label seen? Do not use this to strike any solid object.

On the handle of a hammer

, .

According to a law of Early Renaissance Venice, what must be painted black?

A decree was handed down in 1562 stating only gondola transporting important passengers could be colored, while all others must be black

, .

What was the first U.S. city to put fluoride into their water?

Grand Rapids, Michigan

, .

Which two U.S. Presidents were both born in Vermont?

Chester A. Arthur and Calvin Coolidge

, .

What became the first toy advertised on television in 1952?

Mr. Potato Head

, .

What famous play by Pittsburgh Steelers fullback Franco Harris led to the team's first ever playoff victory in 1972?

The Immaculate Reception

, .

Formed in 1972, the Winnipeg Jets professional hockey team moved, and became what team in 1996?

Arizona Coyotes

, .

What country music star once joined the New York Mets spring training team?

Garth Brooks, he went 0-17 at bat, and was not added to the rotation

, .

What famous Washington, D.C. landmark is British-American Dr. William Thornton best known for designing?

The United States Capitol

, .

During the 1987-'88 NBA season what player was almost traded to the Los Angeles Clippers?

Michael Jordan, for any five Clippers players or draft picks

, .

In July of 2016, Funai Electric of Japan ceased production of what product?

Video cassette recorders (Funai Electric is the last Japanese company to produce VCR units)

, .

What is used to celebrate goals and wins for the Columbus Blue Jackets hockey team?

A replica 1857 Napoleon cannon

, .

In the 1896 Olympic Games, who received medals?

First place won silver, Second won bronze. Three medals were introduced in 1904.

, .

What NBA team has a mascot gorilla nicknamed "Go"?

Phoenix Suns

, .

What NBA team did Julius Erving play for when the video game "One on One: Dr. J vs. Larry Bird" was released?

Philadelphia 76ers

, .

Who actually played the piano in the film "Casablanca"?

The piano playing in the film was performed by Elliot Carpenter, a staff musician, while Dooley Wilson (Sam) fingered the keyboard on camera.

What state has more personalized, or vanity, license plates than any other state?

Illinois, with nearly 1.3 million

, .

What were the Denver Nuggets called when it entered the ABA in 1967?

Denver Rockets

, .

What NASCAR driver won his first race at the 2007 Coca-Cola 600 at Lowe's Motor Speedway?

Casey Mears

, .

What state has more local telephone companies than any other state?

Iowa

, .

What is the largest U.S. city with a one-syllable name?

Flint, Michigan

, .

Since 1996, what is the mascot of the Detroit Pistons?

A horse wearing a Pistons uniform

, .

How did Gutzon Borglum carve Mount Rushmore?

90 % of the mountain was carved with dynamite

, .

What sport features only about 18 minutes of action?

Baseball

, .

New York City's borough the Bronx was named after what European settler?

Jonas Bronck

, .

Though Seattle, Washington is nicknamed "Rain City", what city actually gets more annual precipitation?

Washington, D.C.

, .

What actress had no previous acting experience prior to her role in "The Mask"?

Cameron Diaz

, .

What part of the White House was originally a coat room?

The White House Family Theater

, .

What is the only state that has never had a team in the NCAA Basketball Tournament?

Maine

, .

What pro baseball player had three seasons with over 60 home runs?

Sammy Sosa

, .

Starting in 1990, what NBA team never had a three game losing streak in eight years?

Chicago Bulls

, .

What NFL team has neither hosted or appeared in a Super Bowl?

Cleveland Browns

, .

What tennis player's name can be typed entirely with your left hand?

Federer

, .

At the Sochi Winter Olympics, what country won the most medals?

Russia

, .

Who was the only Pope to retire in the last 600 years?

Benedict XVI

, .

A hologram performance of what deceased singer was featured at the 2014 Billboard Music Awards?

Michael Jackson

, .

What is the 31.4-mile-long rail tunnel linking the United Kingdom with France?

Channel Tunnel

, ·

How do dogs see colors?

Dogs have cone cells in their eyes, which differentiate light or dark on a scale of blue and yellow.

, ·

How many dogs could be produced if a dog is not spayed or neutered?

In six years, a dog could produce about 66,000 puppies.

, ·

How many words and gestures can dogs understand?

They can understand about 250 words and gestures.

, ·

What is the rarest breed of dog?

Cesky Terrier. There are only 350 known to exist.

, ·

How fast do greyhounds run?

Greyhounds can reach speeds over 70 mph.

, •

How quickly can dogs locate the source of a sound?

By using their ears like radar, it takes them about 6/100th of a second to find the source.

, •

How many dog breeds are there?

According to the Fédération Cynologique Internationale (FCI), there are 340 recognized breeds.

, •

Are dogs mentioned in the Holy Bible?

Dogs are mentioned over 40 times. A cat is only mentioned once, in the Book of Baruch.

, •

What is the most popular dog name worldwide?

Max

, •

What pair of actresses looked so much alike in "Star Wars: Episode I - The Phantom Menace" that their own mothers could not tell them apart?

Keira Knightley and Natalie Portman

, .

How many cells are in your body?

The human body contains almost ten trillion cells

, .

93 % of what country's continent is submerged?

New Zealand (Zealandia)

, .

How many people sentenced to death in the U.S. are innocent?

1 in 25 people

, .

Tulsa, Oklahoma was the birthplace of what technological patent?

Gordon Matthews patented Voicemail in 1983

, .

How often do koalas sleep?

20 hours a day

, .

The male of what fish species can release 100-1000 young?

Male sea horse

, .

How much land does the Amazon Rainforest cover?

The Amazon covers 2.1 million square miles

, .

What actress was raised in Nuremberg and grew up speaking German?

Sandra Bullock

, .

What actor's real mother played his character's mother in "General Hospital"?

James Franco

, .

In 1977, what band played its first ever U.S. concert in Austin, Texas?

AC/DC

, .

Drinking two cups of what beverage has been found to drop the risk of suicide by 50%?

Coffee

, .

What does the "D" stand for in D-Day?

"D" stands for Day, H-Hour, means time of operation

, .

How much blood can one pint of blood save?

One pint saves three lives

, .

What actor attained five national titles in Wushu (Chinese combat arts) before becoming a teenager?

Jet Li

, .

What makes water boil and freeze at the same time?

This happens as the temperature and pressure is right for the phases of gas, liquid and solid to "co-exist".

, .

Seriously, which came first the chicken or the egg?

The chicken, because the protein that makes egg shells is only produced by hens

, .

Twitter has how many monthly active users?

Twitter averages at 310 million active users, just under the entire U.S. population.

, .

Why was the DeLorean in "Back to The Future" equipped with a custom speedometer?

A 1979 law prohibited speedometers from going over 85 mph

, .

Stanley Kubrick's film "Full Metal Jacket" was based on what book?

The Short-Timers by Gustav Hasford

, .

Before the symbol of a heart was used to depict love in the 14th century, what represented love?

Foliage (fig leaves)

, .

What scientific method turns venom into painkillers?

Toxineering

, .

How can people double the risk of becoming obese?

By regularly eating breakfast or dinner in restaurants

, .

How many of the last six U.S. Presidents were left handed?

Four (Ronald Reagan, George H.W. Bush, Bill Clinton, and Barack Obama)

, .

Are there volcanoes on planet Venus?

There are more volcanoes on Venus than any other planet in the solar system.

, .

What famous Greek landmark was recreated
for the 1897 World's Fair in Nashville,
Tennessee?

The Parthenon

, .

In Thailand, who is employed as harvesters on
Coconut plantations?

Monkeys

, .

What food was endorsed by the Catholic
Church as a test of conversion from Judaism?

Christmas ham

, .

How many people on Earth use cell phones?

*Out of 6.8 billion people on Earth, 4 billion use cell
phones*

, .

How many prisoners successfully escaped
Auschwitz?

144 prisoners

, .

What concession stand item costs more than filet mignon in the U.S.?

Movie theater popcorn

, .

The world's largest naval base and North American headquarters of NATO are within what city?

Norfolk, Virginia

, .

How do cats mark their scent on people?

With scent glands all over their body, they rub you, and "claim" you as their own

, .

What is the most popular non-chocolate Easter candy?

Marshmallow Peeps. Americans buy over 700 million Peeps during the Easter season.

, .

What do Lionel Richie and Adele have in common?

They both had number one hits titled "Hello".

, .

Microsoft founder Bill Gates dropped out of what college in the 1970s?

Harvard College

, .

What game accessory features voice recognition so you can say "Xbox on." In three languages?

Kinect

, .

What does E=MC2 stand for?

"E" stands for the energy of the object in question. m stands for its mass; and. c stands for the speed of light in vacuum

, .

What organization's officers include a Worshipful Master, Senior Warden, and a Junior Warden?

Masonic Lodge

, .

What university has the largest campus in the U.S.?

Ohio State University

, .

What singer has 7 wax models at the famous Madam Tussauds Museums around the world?

Rihanna

, .

What town in Turkey is known for its underground cities?

Derinkuyu

, .

What U.S. President coined the term "United Nations" in 1942?

Franklin D. Roosevelt

, .

How many words did Arnold Schwarzenegger speak in "Terminator 2: Judgement Day"?

A total of 700 words, including "Hasta la vista, baby".

, .

What has not had a moment off work since you were an embryo?

Your heart

, .

What is the longest east–west interstate highway in the United States?

The longest is I-90 at 3,020.54 miles. It runs from Seattle, Washington to Boston, Massachusetts.

, .

Which two mammals are the only ones that lay eggs?

Duck-billed platypus and Spiny anteater

, .

What is the total weight of all your bones?

15% of your total body weight. If you weigh 100 lbs. your bones weigh about 15lbs.

, .

At the Nakizumo festival in Japan, who competes to make babies cry?

Sumo wrestlers

, .

How much beer is consumed annually at the annual Sturgis Motorcycle Rally?

It is estimated that 3 million gallons of beer is consumed at the South Dakota rally.

, .

What is a hypnagogic myoclonus?

A shock-like jerk or twitch of the body, just before one falls asleep

, .

What rock group recorded a jingle for Kellogg's Rice Krispies in 1964?

The Rolling Stones

, .

What superhero-sidekick was known best for his "Holy" catchphrases?

Batman's trusty comrade Robin (Dick Grayson), played by Burt Ward

, .

What is the brightest star of our night sky called?

Sirius (The Dog star)

, .

Tom Hanks gained 50 pounds and grew d a beard for pre-production of what film?

Cast Away

, .

Does the term "insane" have a medical meaning?

Insanity is purely a legal term, used when a person lacks criminal responsibility for a crime

, .

What skirt-like garment was traditionally worn by Scottish regiments?

Kilt

, .

Which sports car is identified by a raging bull emblem?

Lamborghini

, .

Sir Isaac Newton was featured on what company's first logo?

Apple (The logo depicts Isaac Newton sitting under a tree, an apple dangling precipitously above his head)

, .

In 1978, the young band U2 won a talent contest in Dublin, Ireland, sponsored by what brewery?

Guinness

, .

What company brought back its iconic red stapler after its appearance in the film "Office Space"?

Swingline

, .

What is the average age of a video game player in the United States?

Age 18 to 35

, .

Who spread religion, as well as fruit throughout the Midwestern U.S. in the 1790s?

Johnny Appleseed

, .

What winged horse carried Zeus' thunderbolts?

Pegasus

, .

What was the first solar powered plane to make a round-the-world trip?

Solar Impulse 2. It spent over 23 days in flight, finally landing in Abu Dhabi in July 2016.

, .

Approximately how many actors have portrayed the role of Jesus Christ on television and film combined?

IMDB lists over 600 occurrences of Jesus Christ as a character on TV and film

, .

What former child star became a U.S. Ambassador to Ghana and later to Czechoslovakia?

Shirley Temple

, .

Several years after starring on "Full House", who started the American fashion brand called 'The Row'?

Ashley and Mary-Kate Olsen

, .

What carbonated soft drink is available in over 70 flavors in Japan?

Fanta

, .

What is the only U.S. native animal
with a baby called a joey?

Possum

, .

How many devices were connected to the
internet in 1984?

*There were 1,000 internet devices in 1984, in 2016
there are over 22 billion.*

, .

Who made the first non-stop flight across the
Atlantic Ocean?

British aviators John Alcock and Arthur Brown

, .

What 18th century leader had 600-foot ice
ramps (pre-dating roller coasters) constructed
at their palace?

Catherine the Great

, .

What American singer and actress designed a
line of shoes with famed shoe designer
Giuseppe Zanotti?

Jennifer Lopez

, .

What dance style was popularized by South Korean performer Psy in 2012?

Gangnam Style

, .

What is a perfectly round three-dimensional geometrical object?

Sphere

, .

What was James Patterson's first novel in the 'Alex Cross' series?

Along Came a Spider

, .

In what mountain range is the Donner Pass located?

Sierra Nevada

, .

Who narrated the 1966 Christmas special "Dr. Seuss' How the Grinch Stole Christmas!"?

Boris Karloff

, .

How many glaciers are inside of Glacier National Park in Montana?

There are 25 glaciers today. In 1850, there were 150 in the area.

, .

What comic book character worked for The Daily Star before meeting Clark Kent?

Lois Lane

, .

What was the earliest known literary use of the word 'assassination'?

Macbeth by William Shakespeare (1605)

, .

What Native American tribe opened the first Indian-operated high-stakes bingo hall in the U.S.?

Seminole

, .

At what age did WWE Diva Paige make her professional wrestling debut?

Paige was 13 when she started on the European Independent Circuit. She became the youngest WWE Divas champion at age 21 in 2014.

What is required for all new buildings in San Francisco starting in 2017?

They must have solar panels

, .

What did Jesus Christ look like?

There is no description of his physical appearance in the Holy Bible.

, .

Which MLB player holds the record for most career hits?

Pete Rose (4256 hits)

, .

How many countries in the world were never invaded by the British?

There have only been 22 countries that Britain has not had a military presence.

, .

In 2015 who was named the MVP of the NBA Celebrity All-Star Game for the fourth time?

Kevin Hart

, .

The exterior of what Chicago landmark was used as Wayne Enterprises in "The Dark Knight Rises"?

Trump Tower

, .

How much email per day is actually spam?

45% of all emails per day are spam

, .

What pro athlete pledged $87 million for hometown kids to attend college?

LeBron James

, .

What producer signed novelty music acts such as World Wrestling Foundation, Power Rangers, and Teletubbies?

Simon Cowell

, .

Johnny Depp visits children in hospitals dressed as what movie character?

Captain Jack Sparrow

, .

American columnist John L. O'Sullivan was best known for what term?

Manifest Destiny (the belief that the United States should own all of the land between the Atlantic and Pacific Oceans.)

, .

What American tennis star's father once represented Iran in boxing in the 1948 and 1952 Olympics?

Andre Agassi

, .

What is the most shoplifted food item in the U.S.?

Candy (In Europe, more people shoplift cheese)

, .

50 million people still visit what social networking website every month?

Myspace

, .

What did New York City once use for water mains in the early 19th Century?

Hollowed out trees

What city has the highest population
of the entire United States?

New York City

What NASA explorers are simulating life on
Mars, in what state?

Hawaii (on the Mauna Loa Volcano)

What fruit is known to bounce when it is ripe?

Cranberries

How many balls are on a standard 8-ball pool
table?

*Sixteen (Seven solid colored, Seven striped, an 8-ball,
and a cue ball)*

What occupational hazard affects 25 % of all
computer operators in the United States?

Carpal Tunnel Syndrome

According to research, what group of people have a poor sense of smell?

Psychopaths

, .

What tombstone symbol typically is used for a woman who has died young?

A dove, lying dead

, .

In what year did three people hold the office of President of the United States?

1881 (Rutherford B. Hayes, James Garfield, and Chester A. Arthur)

, .

Ferdinand Magellan started the first voyage of global circumnavigation in 1519. Who finished the voyage in 1522?

Juan Sebastián Elcano

, .

Since 1965, what character has starred in over 600 television commercials?

The Pillsbury Doughboy

, .

What would you be missing without that little pinkie finger on your hand?

People lose about 50% of their hand strength without their pinkie finger.

, .

Almost 90% of Millennials always have what by their side, day and night?

Their smartphone

, .

What restaurant chain was founded by Atari co-founder Nolan Bushnell?

Chuck E. Cheese

, .

What was African-American surgeon Charles Drew best known for?

He discovered blood plasma, and pioneered "blood banks" in World War II.

, .

Who is the only solo female pop singer from the 1990's with a #1 hit in this decade?

Britney Spears

, .

On what date was the seventh album by Styx "The Grand Illusion" released?

July 7, 1977 (7/7/77)

, .

What carbonated soft drink is used as a remedy for indigestion, motion sickness, or sore throats?

Ginger ale

, .

What is the only bird with a beak longer than its body?

Sword-billed hummingbird

, .

What room of the White House was originally a swimming pool?

The media briefing room

, .

How are hurricanes named?

They are named alphabetically, with names familiar to the region, with especially deadly hurricane names retired to avoid confusion.

, .

What song was not added to the film "Grease" until after the film was completed?

"Hopelessly Devoted to You"

, .

Who was Johnny Carson's first guest on "The Tonight Show"?

Groucho Marx

, .

What former "Star Trek" actor served in the U.S. Army from 1953-1955, reaching the rank of Staff Sergeant?

Leonard Nimoy

, .

What weapon was named after the children's book "Thomas A. Swift's electric rifle"?

TASER

, .

What do 42 % of men and women not do after graduating college?

They never read another book

, .

What type of geological era has the earth been in for the past 11,000 years?

Interglacial

, .

What was used to steer the first automobiles?

Levers

, .

Writers are offered free long-distance transportation by what company?

Amtrak

, .

What is the shortest word in the English language that contains the letters ABCDEF?

Feedback

, .

What product marketed by the Wham-O company was banned in Japan, in fear of moral improprieties?

Hula-hoop

, .

How much energy does the Earth get from the sun?

With 12 hours of sun in a day, it equals to 438,000 watt-hours per square foot per year. That's much more than we would use in a year

, .

Who has more churches (and attending members) per capita than any other U.S. state?

Mississippi

, .

What was New Mexico named after?

Nuevo Mexico was given its name in 1563 by Spanish explorers. Mexico was known as New Spain until 1821

, .

On a first date, does it matter where you decide to go?

Choosing an exciting place increases the chance of a second date!

, .

What was the first #1 rap song on the UK music charts?

"Turtle Power" by Partners in Kryme

, .

What archipelago is inside of Puget Sound Washington features nearly 786 islands during low tide?

San Juan Islands

, .

Where is the tallest lighthouse in the United States?

Buxton, North Carolina (Cape Hatteras Lighthouse)

, .

In 2010, what was dropped from the iconic MTV logo?

Music Television

, .

What happens to goldfish if they are kept in a dark room?

They lose some of their pigment, and eventually will start to fade

, .

Trash is converted into heat for almost a million homes in what country?

Sweden

, .

How many episodes of the TV series "Route 66" were actually filmed on Route 66?

None

, .

What children's author was the creator and head writer of the animated series "Eureeka's Castle"?

R.L. Stine

, .

"The Great Gatsby" was penned by what Minnesota native?

F. Scott Fitzgerald

, .

What explorer did native Hawaiians believe was the deity Lono?

Captain James Cook

, .

Which city contains the longest subway system in the world?

Shanghai Metro (588km, 365.4 mi)

, .

What are NFL cheerleaders paid?

Minimum wage

, ·

What synthetic product is chewing gum made from?

Rubber

, ·

In 2002, an Iraqi vice president offered that what two world leaders should fight a duel, to spare the countries from going to war?

Saddam Hussein and George W. Bush

, ·

What company's future was saved in the 1970s by blackjack winnings in Las Vegas?

FedEx

, ·

What was the largest lobster documented?

In Nova Scotia in 1977, a lobster weighed 44 lbs., 6 oz. and was between three and four feet long.

, ·

Where was the first modern shopping cart invented?

Sylvan Goldman owner of the Piggly Wiggly supermarket in Oklahoma City, OK   invented the "folding basket carrier" in 1937.

, .

You've heard of a murder of crows, or flock of ducks, but what bird group is called a pandemonium?

Parrots

, .

687 Earth days encompass a year on what planet?

Mars

, .

What transportation company expects its drivers to pay all expenses for its vehicles?

Uber

, .

Can the Zika virus be spread through sex?

Typically spread by mosquitoes, the Zika virus is also transmitted through sex.

For one year in 1789, what became the first capital of the United States?

New York City

What filmmaker is regarded as "father of the modern zombie films"?

George A. Romero

What NFL team were formerly called the Titans?

The New York Jets were founded as the Titans in 1959 and adopted the Jets as their name in 1963.

What singer had his only number-one hit with the song "My Ding-a Ling" in 1972?

Chuck Berry

What is the robe that Japanese geishas traditionally wear called?

Kimono

August 30, 2011 was proclaimed as what holiday in the state of North Dakota?

Mr. Bubble Day, celebrating the bubble bath product's North Dakota heritage.

In 1807, what emperor was attacked by rabbits?

Napoleon

During the 1995 and 2011 earthquakes in Japan, who notably provided aid quicker than the Japanese government?

The Yakuza, Japan's largest organized crime syndicate

A gigantic. unfinished memorial carved in a mountain in the Black Hills of South Dakota depicts what native warrior?

Crazy Horse

In the 1940s, what Nobel prize winning author was placed under surveillance by the FBI?

Ernest Hemingway

Filmation used bodybuilders as a reference for animating what 1980s cartoon?

He-Man and the Masters of the Universe

What is the number one cause of chronic depression?

Fear-based, negative thinking.

What college football players are typically picked earlier in the NFL draft, and paid more?

"Team players" who put their teammates first

What is the largest crab in the world?

Coconut crab. It can weigh up to 4.1 kg (9.0 lb) and 1 m (3 ft 3 in) in length from leg to leg.

How much was the average cost of a 30-second commercial during Super Bowl I in 1967?

The cost was $37,500. By Super Bowl XLIX in 2015, the price was around $4.5 million.

How fast is a bullet from a .22 caliber rifle?

1,400 to 1,800 feet per second

What happens to astronauts' hearts in space?

For long periods at zero gravity, their hearts lose muscle mass, and actually become more spherical.

What destroyed over 80 % of the San Francisco area in 1906?

A 7.8 magnitude earthquake, which killed over 3,000 people

Can the federal government read your emails without a warrant?

The U.S. government does not require a warrant to access emails which are more than 180 days old.

Nearly 2,300 people were shot and killed in what city in 2016?

Chicago, Illinois

What agency handles almost half of the world's mail volume?

United States Postal Service

What famous American soldier was selected for the first-ever modern pentathlon for the 1912 Olympic Games in Stockholm, Sweden?

George S. Patton

What is the length of the U.S.-Canadian border, excluding Alaska?

About 3,987 miles

In 1977, the body of famous actor was stolen, and held for ransom just two months after he died?

Charlie Chaplin

What product has photographed over 5 million miles of road for its 'street view' maps?

Google

What country has the tallest people?

*Dutch men, at about 6 feet, and Latvian women at 5' 7"
are the tallest in the world*

**In 2015, how much of the city of London's
population were not natives?**

*37 % of London's population were born outside the
UK.*

How can you tell how ripe a watermelon is?

*The "ground spot" should be yellow. If it is white or
green, it may have been picked too soon.*

**A first baseman in 1875, donned a pair of
flesh-colored what, so fans wouldn't notice
him wearing them?**

Baseball gloves

**How can you get an official pirate certificate
at the Massachusetts Institute of Technology
(MIT)?**

Students who complete courses in pistol, archery, sailing, and fencing is considered a pirate.

What is the flattest state in the U.S.?

Florida

, .

Who invented the jumping jack exercise?

John J. Pershing, an army general at West Point

, .

What is the world's smallest movie titled?

IBM Research filmed 'A Boy and His Atom' was made by moving atoms and shot with a special tunneling microscope.

, .

What computer had less power than that of a modern calculator or cell phone?

The computer that landed Apollo 11 on the moon

, .

What is inscribed on the Statue of Liberty's tablet?

The tablet reads: July IV, MDCCLXXVI. It is the date the Declaration of Independence.

In what year did the Olympic Games feature a pigeon shooting event?

The 1900 Olympic Games

In the 30th Miss USA pageant, why was Deborah Fountain of New York disqualified?

She padded her swimsuit

What animal is responsible for deaths of over 1 million people every year?

Mosquitos

What Greek scholar first determined the circumference of the Earth?

Eratosthenes, the Father of Geography

What is the temperature of the surface of the sun?

The surface is about 10,000 degrees F (5,500 degrees C). At the core, the temperature can reach 27 million degrees F (15 million degrees C).

What city boasts the largest municipal park system in the United States?

Philadelphia's Fairmount Park. With 9,200 acres, It's larger than New York City's Central Park.

How does insect repellent with DEET work?

The chemicals in DEET jams the insect's odor receptors

What word means "empty orchestra" in Japanese?

Karaoke

Who launched the "Great Building Campaign" during the Great Depression, substituting the power of steam shovels with men?

Milton Hershey

What country is moving northward at 5.6 cm per year?

Australia

What is the fear of dental care called?

Odontophobia

Tigers have never been native to what country?

Africa

What causes the air to smell differently after it rains?

Bacteria called actinomycetes causes the odor with rain. The smell is called petrichor.

The human nose is capable of smelling how many different smells?

We can distinguish 1 trillion different odors

What Russian emperor finally abolished serfdom in 1861?

Alexander II

What two competing shoe companies were founded by brothers?

Adidas was founded by Adolf Dassler, while Puma was founded by his brother Rudi.

, .

The three-finger salute of "Hunger Games" is used by anti-military protesters in what country?

Thailand

, .

What is the steam train in Scotland known as the Hogwarts Express from the "Harry Potter" film series?

The Jacobite

, .

Amanita muscaria mushrooms were the basis of what video game's power-up items?

Super Mario Bros.

, .

Teams of six wearing flippers and snorkels wrestle with a ball in a pool in what sport?

Underwater Rugby

, .

What is a polygon with 30 sides called?

Triacontagon

, .

When Alicia Keys played June Boatwright in "The Secret Life of Bees", what instrument did she learn to play in four weeks?

She learned to play cello in four weeks.

, .

What did the city of Hot Springs, New Mexico change its name to in 1950?

Truth or Consequences

, .

How long is the average gestation for giraffe?

About 15 months

, .

A sculpture of a 13-foot middle finger was erected in front of what building in 2010?

Italian artist Maurizio Cattelan's marble sculpture sits in front of Milan's Italian Stock Exchange building.

, .

What city has the most Rolls-Royce luxury cars per capita?

Hong Kong

, .

Who was responsible for producing the opening and closing ceremonies of the1960 Winter Olympics?

Walt Disney

, .

What person had the longest name in the Holy Bible?

Mahershalalhashbaz

, .

Due to its high pollution levels, what is breathing the air for one day in Mumbai equivalent to?

It is equivalent to 100 cigarettes a day

, .

Who was chairman of Walt Disney Studios from 1984-1994, then co-founded Dreamworks SKG with Steven Spielberg?

Jeffrey Katzenberg

, .

Who led the first public
anti-smoking campaign?

Nazi Germany

, .

How many McDonald's restaurants are
located in the United States?

*There are 14,248 McDonald's locations. That is almost
9,000 more McDonald's than there are hospitals.*

, .

How long would it take for a snail to circle
Earth?

It would take a snail over 4,500 years to circle Earth

, .

Who made the historic first phone call to the
moon?

President Richard Nixon, July 20, 1969

, .

All of what region of the world have crosses
on their flags?

Scandanavia

, .

What creature have scientists discovered that can live forever?

Turritopsis dohrnii, a jellyfish

, ·

According to a survey, how many teen drivers use cell phone apps while driving?

Nearly 70% use apps while driving.

, ·

Why didn't telephone inventor Alexander Graham Bell ever call his wife or mother?

They were both deaf

, ·

What activity is ten times more effective as a tranquilizer than Valium?

Sex

, ·

Who became president under the Articles of Confederation in 1781, making him the 1st U.S. President?

John Hanson

, ·

Before rubber erasers, what
material was used?

Crustless bread

, .

What caused the deaths of four million people
in Indonesia?

*Famine and forced labor during the Japanese
occupation of World War 2*

, .

Facing forward in a ship, what are the nautical
terms for left and right?

Port is left. Starboard is right.

, .

What was the last country to win the Olympic
Gold Medal in rugby?

*The United States defeated France 17-3 at the 1924
Summer Olympics.*

, .

In the contiguous United States, which state
has the longest coastline?

*Florida, 1,350 miles (3,496 km) Atlantic Ocean and
Gulf of Mexico*

, .

What do 44 % of kids do before going to sleep?

Watch television

, .

Days and nights have equal periods of sunlight and darkness on what annual astronomical event?

Equinox, Vernal equinox (March) or Autumnal equinox (September)

, .

What did scientists create in 1997 to illustrate nanotechnology?

The fully functioning nano guitar. It is the size of an average red blood cell.

, .

What is regulation height for a basketball hoop?

10 feet, from the ground to the top of the rim.

, .

According to a documentary, what revolutionary leader claimed he slept with 35,000 women?

Former Cuban President Fidel Castro

, .

What is the scientific term for the type of tickling that makes you laugh and squirm?

Gargalesis makes you laugh and squirm. Light tickling such as a feather on the skin is called knismesis.

, .

What Australian lizard drinks water through condensation in its skin?

Thorny devil

, .

What cold product neutralizes the heat from eating spicy food?

Ice cream

, .

In the next version of the iPhone operating system, what controversial emoji was replaced?

The pistol emoji was replaced with a green water gun

, .

What is German Chancellor Angela Merkel's trademark hand gesture called?

Merkel diamond

, .

When did the White House first celebrate Independence Day?

In 1801, President Thomas Jefferson held the first 4th of July event

, .

Why is Elvis Presley's middle name spelled Aron?

In honor of his twin brother, Jesse Garon Presley who died at birth

, .

How many lakes are in Minnesota?

Although the state's nickname says "Land of 10,000 Lakes", there are actually 11,842 lakes that are 10 acres or larger.

, .

For their aid in World War II, the Netherlands sends 20,000 tulip bulbs to what country?

Canada

, .

What are young rabbits called?

Kittens

, .

How many patents did Thomas Edison claim around the world?

He accumulated 2,332 patents for his inventions.

, .

What food causes the most choking for children under age 14?

Hot dogs. 17% of food-related choking deaths are caused by hot dogs.

, .

What is the fastest goal in the history of professional soccer?

In 2009, a Saudi Arabian player scored two seconds after the opening whistle.

, .

What is the fastest car in the world?

Bugatti Veyron Super Sport at 269.86mph

, .

Who did NBC Chairman Robert Greenblatt claim would not be welcome to host "The Celebrity Apprentice"?

Donald Trump

, .

In what started as an accident, how many guitars did The Who's Pete Townshend destroy in 1967?

According to analysis, he broke more than 35 guitars in 1967.

, .

What type of car was used in the films "Jackie Brown", "Pulp Fiction", and "Kill Bill: Volume 2"?

A white Honda Civic

, .

How much of America believes that climate change will pose a serious threat in their life?

62% of Americans don't think climate change is a threat.

, .

Who sought the nomination for U.S. President three times and failed, and declined the offer for vice-presidency twice?

Daniel Webster

, .

What is Donald Duck's middle name?

Fauntleroy (a reference to his sailor hat)

How long can a human live without food?

Experts claim the human body can survive for up to two months, depending on their overall health and mental state.

, .

How did American Airlines save over $40,000 in 1987?

By removing one olive from their salads.

, .

Who trademarked several phrases like 'This Sick Beat' and 'Party Like It's 1989" in 2015?

Taylor Swift. The phrases are from her album "1989".

, .

What is the fictional city of Great Britain where King Arthur held court?

Camelot

, .

How many countries do not have a McDonald's restaurant?

As of 2013, there were over 100 countries without McDonald's.

, .

In 2014, how many house fires occurred in the U.S.?

There was one house fire reported every 86 seconds

, .

Scientists have recently discovered the rare and endangered Araguaian boto in Brazil. What is it?

A river dolphin

, .

What is the time for light to travel from the sun to Earth?

It takes an average 8 minutes and 20 seconds.

, .

In what country does your income have a factor in how much your traffic ticket will cost?

Finland. Fines are also based on the severity of the offense.

, .

What animal swims 5,000 miles every year to reunite with the man who saved his life in 2011?

A South American Magellanic penguin

, •

What was the first major Hollywood film to be filmed entirely in digital video?

Star Wars: Episode II – Attack of the Clones

, •

Who is the only NFL quarterback to win a playoff game over the age of 40?

Brett Favre

, •

What historical feat was accomplished by the U.S. nuclear submarine Nautilus in 1958?

The first undersea voyage to the geographic North Pole, where it reached the top of the world.

, •

What Greek mathematician used mirrors and the sun's reflection to destroy enemy ships attacking Syracuse?

Archimedes

, •

Where did the television series "Little House On the Prairie" take place?

Walnut Grove, Minnesota

, ·

Do all spiders build webs?

All spiders make silk, but not all spiders make webs

, ·

To help the country's climate change, what record breaking achievement did 800,000 volunteers do in India in 2016?

They planted 50 million trees in 1 day

, ·

What composition was the theme music for the television program "Alfred Hitchcock Presents"?

The Funeral March of a Marionette by Charles Gounod

, ·

In World War I, what was used for air to air combat before guns were installed?

They threw bricks, grenades, rope, and eventually used pistols and carbines.

, ·

In the game baseball for the blind 'Beep Baseball', what players are not blind?

The pitcher and catcher

, .

What happens to pre-printed losing sports team's championship stuff?

The World Vision organization collects pre-printed loser gear such as hats and shirts and donate about $2 million worth of items to poor countries per year.

, .

What is the mascot of the Baltimore Ravens?

Poe, named after writer and Baltimore resident, Edgar Allan Poe.

, .

While most 13th-15th century English commoners spoke English, what language was spoken by British elites?

French

, .

During the 1930s 'Dust Bowl' era, when money was tight, what was used for clothing?

Flour sacks

Who was America's first slave owner?

A black man named Anthony Johnson, who owned white slaves.

, .

What common item may have more bacteria than toilet seats?

Office desks

, .

What significant event occurred in Game 1 of the 1918 World Series?

It marked the first time "The Star Spangled Banner" was performed at a major league game.

, .

Pieces of the Berlin Wall decorate the walls of what building in Las Vegas, Nevada?

The main floor men's room of the Main Street Station Casino

, .

What has made daily parades through the Memphis, Tennessee Peabody Hotel lobby since 1930?

Five Mallard ducks

Where is the oldest continuously occupied European-established settlement in the contiguous United States?

St. Augustine, Florida

, .

Why does your skin wrinkle up like a raisin after swimming?

The skin's natural skin lubricant-sebum is temporarily removed, or washed away.

, .

What actor portrayed the fictional character John Munch in nine different television shows on five networks?

Richard Belzer

, .

What player never stepped into the National Baseball Hall of Fame museum until he was elected, because of superstition?

Ken Griffey Jr.

, .

What have researchers found out about the continuous use of Facebook?

The more someone uses it, the more depressed they become

, .

In the 1980s, the Soviet Union traded 17 submarines, a cruiser, a frigate and a destroyer, in exchange for what?

Pepsi products

, .

Where are the most tornadoes in the United States?

Oklahoma has about 52 tornadoes per year and Texas sees about 126 per year.

, .

What has the biggest eyes of any living creature?

Giant and colossal squids

, .

What practice was illegal until 1937 in Atlantic City, New Jersey?

Bare-chested men could not be on the beach.

What is the largest single living organism on Earth?

A mushroom in Oregon's Malheur National Forest has a root system that covers over 2,200 acres.

, .

How effective are boxing gloves?

Boxing gloves add 10 pounds to the weight of a fist, making a punch more lethal.

, .

In 1859, London, England installed the first public water fountain. For the next 50 years, what did people use to drink from it?

A metal cup attached to the fountain by a chain

, .

What car manufacturer was the main sponsor of the television show "Mister Ed"?

Studebaker.

, .

What store in Burbank, California was the filmed location of an unauthorized soap opera spoof?

IKEA. "Ikea Heights" was filmed inside the store without management permission.

The proverbial "see no evil, hear no evil, speak no evil" monkeys first appeared where?

A 17th century carving by Hidari Jongoro

, .

Who invented grape juice?

Dr. Thomas Welch invented a pasteurization process for the prevention of the fermentation of grape juice in 1869.

, .

What country has the highest gas prices, as of August 2016?

Hong Kong, $7.12 per gallon

, .

Since its debut in 1964, how many G.I. Joe figures have been sold?

400 million of the Hasbro action figures have been sold.

, .

What company introduced the first portable electric drill in 1946?

Black & Decker

, .

What is the world's most expensive beer?

Sapporo Space Barley, $110 per six pack

, .

What Olympic teams will stay on the Silver Cloud cruise ship rather than the Olympic Village for the 2016 Summer Olympics?

U.S. men's and women's basketball teams

, .

What is the $20 million reward for privately funded spacecraft to land on the moon by December 31, 2016?

Google Lunar XPRIZE

, .

Prior to his career in The Monkees, Davy Jones starred in what Broadway musical?

Oliver!

, .

From 1930 to 1970, over 85 million American schoolchildren learned to read using what book series?

Dick and Jane

What was tested in China to avoid the unpredictable traffic?

The Transit Elevated Bus

, .

The Hotel Arbez straddles what international border?

France and Switzerland

, .

What gives bones strength and flexibility?

The combination of calcium and collagen

, .

How do you put out a fire in a race car?

Race cars have two extinguishers, one for the driver, one for the fuel cell

, .

Over 5 million trees canopy 25 % of what city?

New York City

, .

What Christmas song was quickly renamed, when the writer was informed of its other meaning?

"Silver Bells" started out as "Tinkle Bells".

, .

What percentage of U.S. adults are cigarette smokers?

About 17% of adults 18 or older smoke cigarettes

, .

When did the ferris wheel debut?

It was debuted at the 1893 Chicago World's Fair

, .

What company had a line of bicycles between 1917 and 1922?

Harley Davidson. The bicycles were built for Harley-Davidson by the Davis Machine Company in Dayton, Ohio.

, .

After World War II, there were more of what classic weapon in the United States than Japan?

Samurai swords

Which was named first, orange (color), or orange (fruit)?

The color orange was named after the fruit.

, .

Which college football bowl game was originally called the "Battle of Flowers"?

The Rose Bowl

, .

What do crocodiles do to digest food better, and dive deeper in lakes and rivers?

They swallow stones

, .

What accident caused Percy Spencer's invention of the microwave oven?

The chocolate bar in his pocket melted from the radiation of a magnetron tube.

, .

What insect is known to sting more than once, since it doesn't lose its stinger?

Yellowjackets

, .

How many kinds of woodpeckers are there?

There are over 180 to 200 species of woodpeckers

, .

What artist hated painting so much, he wrote a poem about what became his most famous piece?

Michelangelo wrote a poem about painting the ceiling of the Sistine Chapel

, .

What form of entertainment can speed up growth of plants?

Playing music speeds up germination of plants

, .

The fictional bridges on Euro currency have been built for real in what country?

Netherlands

, .

Jewish immigrants helped what musician buy his first horn?

Louis Armstrong

, .

What Latin phrase means something for something?

Quid pro quo

, .

How many buffaloes have lived in North America?

None. Early explorers of America called the bison buffaloes because they looked like water buffaloes. In 1883, there were almost 40 million bison in North America.

, .

Who left for London in 1724 to train as a printer?

Benjamin Franklin

, .

How many cases of sexually transmitted diseases are reported in the U.S. each year?

110 million

, .

What video game character's name was inspired by that of an angry landlord?

Nintendo's Mario

What is Lady Gaga's real name?

Stefani Joanne Angelina Germanotta

, ·

What three fruits are native to North America?

Blueberries, cranberries, and Concord grapes

, ·

Wolverine has no lines of dialogue in what "X-Men" movie?

X-Men: Apocalypse

, ·

What creature found on the sides of boats or whales is related to crabs and lobsters?

Barnacles

, ·

During the 1936 Olympic Games, what brand of shoes were worn by Jesse Owens?

Adidas

, ·

Who received the Grammy Award for Best Spoken Word Album in 1997?

Hillary Clinton, for "It Takes a Village: And Other Lessons Children Teach Us"

, .

What character in the Star Trek Universe was played by actor John de Lancie?

Q

, .

What festival has occured on the last Wednesday in August since 1945 in Bunol, Spain?

La Tomatina, a tomato throwing festival

, .

What was the first medical X-Ray by discoverer Wilhelm Rontgen?

His wife's hand

, .

Before George W. Bush met Bono of U2, who did he think Bono was?

Sonny Bono, the American singer who was half of Sonny and Cher

Who was Leonardo da Vinci's subject in the painting "Mona Lisa"?

Lisa Gherardini, the wife of a wealthy silk merchant

, •

On an iPhone how can you delete text?

Shake your phone, and hit undo

, •

How many plants live in Central Africa?

More than 8,000 different known species of plants.

, •

What insect was thought to be extinct by 1920, only to be rediscovered in 2001?

Lord Howe Island stick insect (Dryococelus australis)

, •

What state's name is based on the Caddo word tejas meaning "friends" or "allies"?

Texas

, •

How much money is in a regular Monopoly game?

The bank in a standard game of Monopoly has $15,140 in cash

, .

How much water is in an adult man's body?

About 60% of an adult's bodies are water

, .

Is there a law against lying in the news?

In the U.S., there is no rule against distorting or falsifying the news

, .

How much shoreline does Lake Superior contain?

2,726 miles of shoreline

, .

What talk show hostess set up a 'Hurricane Katrina' relief fund, that raised seven million dollars?

Ellen DeGeneres

, .

How much skin do people have?

An average adult's skin would cover 22 square feet

, .

How many natural elements are there?

Scientists have identified 92 elements.

, .

What pilot revived his own feat of breaking the sound barrier in 2012?

Chuck Yeager

, .

For 24 straight hours on January 23, 1991, what song did the owner of KLSK FM in Albuquerque, New Mexico play?

Led Zeppelin -Stairway to Heaven

, .

Who invented the digital circuit – the foundation that provides us access to the Internet today?

Claude Shannon, the Father of Information Theory

, .

Could spacecraft ever collide with asteroids?

The huge asteroid belt is not so densely populated with asteroids, so the chance of an actual collision would be less than one in a billion.

, .

How much of the world's money is accessed in electronic bank accounts?

92% of the world's currency is digital

, .

What small mountain chain extends from South Dakota to Wyoming?

Black Hills

, .

Sony's Playstation was turned down by what company to compete with Nintendo?

SEGA

, .

In what military branch did Alex Haley, author of "Roots", serve as a journalist?

U.S. Coast Guard

, .

How much do camels drink?

Camels can drink 30 gallons of water in about 13 minutes. Water is stored in their bloodstream.

, .

How many countries border China?

14 countries border China. (India, Pakistan, Afghanistan, Tajikistan, Kyrgyzstan, Kazakhstan, Mongolia, Russia, North Korea, Vietnam, Laos, Myanmar, Bhutan, and Nepal)

, .

The Holy Bible is available in how many languages?

The full Bible has been translated into nearly 3,000 languages, including fictional languages such as Klingon, from "Star Trek".

, .

What insect is considered Kosher in Judaism?

Locust

, .

What famous American author invented the bra-strap clasp?

Mark Twain

In 1988, actor Mark Wahlberg served 45 days in prison for what crime?

Attempted murder

, .

In what country are the people identified as Basotho, and speak a language called Sesotho?

Lesotho, South Africa

, .

What part of a cat's body contains almost 10 percent of the bones in its body?

Its tail

, .

1 percent of the ocean floor is covered by what ecosystem?

Coral reef

, .

What search engine was originally nicknamed "BackRub"?

Google

, .

What famous cyclist, known for a doping scandal, donated over $100,000 in 2002 to fight against doping?

Lance Armstrong

, .

What is the fear that a duck or goose is watching you called?

Anatidaephobia

, .

What is the second largest buyer of explosives in the U.S., after the Department of Defense?

Walt Disney World

, .

100 people choke to death every year on what?

Ballpoint pens

, .

What singer opened a restaurant in 2011 called Soul Kitchen where customers pay what they can or volunteer to earn a meal?

Jon Bon Jovi

, .

What is equipped in Dutch police
cars to comfort children?

Teddy bears

, .

In "The Wizard of Oz", what was the Cowardly
Lion's costume made of?

It was made from real lion skin and fur. The costume
sold at an auction in 2014 for $3 million.

, .

What is the only state whose official drink is
an alcoholic beverage?

Alabama. Conecuh Ridge Whiskey

, .

Since it was introduced in 1963, how many
people have claimed the title of WWE World
Heavyweight Champion?

There have been 32 championship holders.

, .

How many people are aged 100 years or older
in the world today?

About 300,000

, .

How often do we dream?

People typically dream four to six times in one night.

, .

How many towns in the world are named Hell?

Four- 2 in the U.S.- Hell, Michigan and the abandoned Hell, California and one in Norway, also Hel, Poland.

, .

What animal is capable of cleaning its own ears with its tongue?

A giraffe, with its 21-inch tongue

, .

What animal was awarded knighthood by the Norwegian Royal Guard?

Sir Nils Olav, a king penguin at Edinburgh Zoo, Scotland.

, .

What work of art did a woman pay $10,000 for from the Museum of Non-Visible Art in 2011?

It was a non-visible piece, titled "Fresh Air".

, .

Which fraternal organization is referred to as
"the craft"?

Freemasonry

, .

What product did Bayer sell in the 1890s as a
cold and cough remedy?

Heroin

, .

What is the meaning of the French expression
"C'est la vie"?

That's life

, .

In "How the Grinch Stole Christmas!", how
long did the Grinch put up with the Who's
celebration of Christmas?

He put up with it for 53 years

, .

What modern character shares his name with
a character in Nathanael West's 1939 novel
"The Day of the Locusts"?

Homer Simpson

In the movie "The Godfather", what color is strongly associated with the death of many of its characters?

Orange

, .

What was the alternate title of the 1993 film "Hocus Pocus" in many countries outside the U.S.?

Abracadabra!

, .

How many eggs can snails lay per cycle?

Garden snails lay around 80 eggs

, .

How many Americans have hypertension (high blood pressure)?

Over 70 million. 1 in every 3 American adults

, .

How many Americans have myopia (nearsightedness)?

At least 41 percent of Americans are nearsighted.

, .

What U.S. state was the first to make marijuana illegal?

California banned marijuana in 1913

, .

Are all fingerprints unique?

Yes. even twins do not have the same fingerprints.

, .

Why do people refer to Australia as "Down under"?

The country is in the Southern hemisphere, below most others in the world.

, .

What emperor once lined his soldiers along the beach to battle Neptune, and demanded they collect seashells as booty?

Caligula

, .

In 1920, what city had the first commercial radio station?

Pittsburgh, Pennsylvania was home to KDKA.

, .

U.S. athlete Michael Phelps has won a total of 77 medals in what sport?

Swimming (22 medals in the Olympics)

, .

What did Tim Berners-Lee invent in 1989 at the physics laboratory CERN??

The World Wide Web

, .

An adult mouse has how many teeth?

Sixteen teeth

, .

How much milk does a cow produce in one day?

One dairy cow produces about 22.5 quarts of milk per day

, .

After donating blood, how long does it take to recover?

It takes about 48 hours for your body to replace plasma volume.

, .

How old was Pope Benedict IX when he was first elected in 1032?

He was age 12

, .

In 1947, what became the first animals sent into space, in a U.S.-launched V-2 rocket?

Fruit flies

, .

What trait is unique about the Rhinella proboscidea toad?

It is the only species of toad to practice necrophilia.

, .

In 1783, who were the first passengers on a hot-air-balloon?

A sheep, a duck and a rooster

, .

Who introduced the first known ice cream recipe recorded in America?

President Thomas Jefferson

, .

What bioluminescent creature oozes cyanide to warn predators?

Motyxia millipede

, .

What is most of human feces made of?

Feces are made up of 75 percent water and 25 percent solid matter

, .

Who wrote the Johnny Cash hit song "A Boy Named Sue"?

Children's author Shel Silverstein

, .

What did Tim Burton almost release as a sequel for "Beetlejuice"?

Beetlejuice Goes Hawaiian

, .

What television show featured the first on-screen pregnancy?

I Love Lucy. 71.7% of all American TVs were tuned in to see the birth of Desi, Jr.

, .

How many breaths do hmans take in one day?

About 23,000 breaths a day

, •

What country has the largest population of any country in the world?

China. The population is about 1,400,000,000 people

, •

What serial killer's last words "Just Do It" inspired one of Nike's greatest marketing campaigns ever?

Gary Gilmore

, •

What is Broadway's longest-running show and musical?

The Phantom of the Opera 1988-

, •

What are those weird spots you see when you look in the sky for a long time?

White blood cells. It is called blue field entoptic phenomenon

, •

Where did the name cappuccino come from?

The name is from the color of the Capuchin monk's clothing

, .

How much saliva do humans produce every day?

About six cups.

, .

Where is the largest concentration of snakes in the world?

Narcisse Snake Pits, Manitoba, Canada

, .

Can laughter burn calories?

10 to 15 minutes of laughing a day can burn up to 40 calories.

, .

What continent gets the least amount of rain per year?

Antarctica (6.5 inches of rain per year)

, .

Did dinosaurs and humans ever coexist?

No. The last dinosaurs died 65 million years ago. Our earliest human ancestors were 6 million years ago.

, .

From 1951 to 1992, what was located 65 miles north of Las Vegas, Nevada?

A nuclear weapon test site

, .

What method of capital punishment was conceived by a dentist named Alfred P. Southwick?

Electric chair

, .

What is used for the soft textured chocolate between the wafers inside a Kit Kat candy bar?

Mashed up Kit Kats.

, .

What is Japan using to clean up nuclear waste after the tsunami?

Sunflowers

, .

What is the most expensive structure ever built?

The International Space Station ($150 billion)

, .

What is the name of the man on Pringles potato chip cans?

Julius

, .

What movie's special effects included a 1/12 scale White House explosion?

Independence Day. It was one of the last films to use minimal CGI.

, .

What NFL quarterback was drafted as a catcher by the Montreal Expos in the 1995 MLB draft?

Tom Brady

, .

What does Taylor Swift keep in an aquarium in her living room?

Old baseballs

, .

Were George Washington's dentures wooden?

His dentures were constructed of materials including bone, ivory, human teeth, brass screws, and metal wire.

, .

Thanks to the Sprinkles company, what can people do to satisfy their sweet tooth?

They have a 24-hour cupcake ATM which dispenses cupcakes and cookies

, .

Over 150 million pounds of what food product were purchased by the U.S. military during World War II?

Spam

, .

What is the fear of thunder and lightning?

Astraphobia

, .

How big is a blue whale's tongue?

Their tongues can weigh as much as an elephant and their hearts are about the size of a car.

, .

Where is the world's largest collection of comic books?

The Library of Congress in Washington, D.C

, .

What product does Fazoli's restaurant make more than 100 million of every year?

Breadsticks

, .

How much coffee do Americans drink per day?

Americans drink 400 million cups of coffee per day

, .

What part of National Hockey League safety equipment was not used full-time until 1959?

Goalie Mask

, .

How much do Americans spend on gasoline annually?

Americans spend about $3,000 per year on gasoline

, .

What identification method did police use prior to fingerprinting?

The Bertillon system (Bone measurements)

, .

Can dolphins choose to stop breathing?

Every breath they take is a conscious effort. In captivity, dolphins have been known to stop breathing, ending their life in suicide.

, .

What was the fastest mobile game to reach 10 million downloads worldwide?

'Pokemon Go!' It earned nearly $200 million in July 2016 its first month of release.

, .

In 1901, Annie Edson Taylor became the first person to do what?

She went over Niagara Falls in a barrel.

, .

A bronze statue of what philosopher sits in New York City's Chinatown?

Confucius

, .

How long does it take for Mercury to complete a single orbit the sun?

88 days

, .

How far can humans see?

The farthest object is the Andromeda galaxy which is 2.6 million light years from Earth.

, .

What country did Prime Minister Winston Churchill plan to invade with "Operation Unthinkable"?

Soviet Union

, .

What is considered the most poisonous tree in the world?

Manchineel tree

, .

What is the U.S. Department of Defense foreign policy called CONPLAN 8888 for?

A "zombie survival plan"

, .

What was the first commercial use of aluminum foil in the U.S.?

A wrapper for Life Savers candy

, .

Prior to his life a famous occultist, who was a well-known mountain climber?

Aleister Crowley

, .

What animal can last longer without drinking water than a camel?

Giraffe. They can go 3 weeks without a drink.

, .

How big is the Milky Way Galaxy?

100,000 light years in diameter

, .

To catch up their outdated Julian calendar, what day was added to the calendars of Finland and Sweden in 1712?

February 30. In 1753, Sweden changed to the Gregorian calendar by removing 11 days.

, .

What is the fastest human sense?

Hearing. Humans recognize sound in just 0.05 seconds.

, .

A celebration of the marriage of Bavarian King Ludwig I and Maria Theresia in 1810 became known as what?

Oktoberfest

, .

According to Ancient Roman legend, Rome was founded by Romulus and Remus, who were the twin sons of what god?

Mars, the god of War

, .

During World War II, what symbol did Nazis order Jews to wear on their clothing for identification?

A yellow Star of David

, .

While studying at Harvard, who was rejected by the all-female committee to appear in a Black pin-up calendar?

Barack Obama

What became the official flower of the city of Hiroshima after the 1945 bombing?

Oleander. It was the first to bloom after the explosion.

, .

What spider's venom triggers a long lasting, painful erection?

Brazilian wandering spider

, .

What was finally legalized in Japan in 2015, after 67 years?

Late night dancing

, .

What country uses the most ecstasy, according to the World Drug Report?

Australia

, .

What can scent do for our brains?

Memories triggered by scent have a stronger, lasting effect.

, .

Mexican drug cartels earn about $152 million per year from the sale of what fruit?

Avocados

, .

Who designed the prototype for the Atari video game "Breakout"?

Steve Wozniak and Steve Jobs

, .

What pharmaceutical giant carried out medical experiments on Auschwitz prisoners during World War II?

Bayer

, .

How many abortions occur in the U.S. every year?

About 1 million abortions per year

, .

What animal has the longest childhood of any other in the world?

Orangutans. Baby orangutans nurse until they are six years old.

, .

What country has military-style boot camps for those who are addicted to the internet?

China

, .

As of 2015, what country has the largest population in the European Union?

Germany (2015 population: 81,197,537)

, .

What Italian artist and scientist first explained why the sky is blue?

Leonardo da Vinci

, .

What emits more methane than the oil industry?

Livestock such as cattle, pigs, and other animals which produce over 13 million tons of methane.

, .

What country receives $3.1 million annually in foreign aid from the U.S?

Israel

, .

What is a bigger health crisis
than hunger in the world?

*More people in the world suffer from obesity than from
hunger.*

, .

What actor rejoined the New York Fire
Department after 9/11 to sift through the
rubble from the World Trade Center attacks?

Steve Buscemi

, .

Eleven of the twelve men who did what were
boy scouts?

They walked on the moon

, .

What author carried his first pages of "The
Catcher in the Rye" as he stormed the
beaches of Normandy in World War II?

J. D. Salinger

, .

From 1513 to 1972, what was every Danish king
alternately named?

Frederick or Christian

What green spirit was once banned in several countries for being addictive and hallucinogenic?

Absinthe

, •

The largest wingspan belongs to what bird?

The wandering albatross (8 ft 3 in to 11 ft 6 in.)

, •

What are the five dwarf planets of our solar system?

Pluto, Ceres, Eris, Haumea, and Makemake

, •

What area of the world contains nearly 20 million tons of gold?

In the ocean

, •

What is the comic character Andy Capp known as in Germany?

Willi Wakker

, •

The 1972 album by Carl and the Passions titled "So Tough" was actually performed by what band?

The Beach Boys

، .

What was the top selling item at Wal-Mart prior to Hurricane Frances in 2004?

Beer

، .

What dinosaur was considered the biggest that ever existed?

Seismosaurus

، .

What president was on the $1,000 bill?

Grover Cleveland

، .

How many kangaroos live in Australia?

About 50 to 60 million kangaroos

، .

In World War I, who became known as the 'canary girls'?

Women who worked with TNT suffered jaundice

, .

Where do most roses sold on Valentine's Day in the U.S. come from?

South America

, .

How much caffeine is in a chocolate bar?

A 1-ounce chocolate bar has about 5 milligrams of caffeine.

, .

What did Rabbi Yaacov Deyo create in 1998 to help Jewish singles meet and marry?

Speed dating

, .

According to the National Safety Council, what youth sport has caused the most injuries?

Basketball

, .

How can you guess the age of a lion?

The color of their nose. The noses turn from pink to black as they age.

, .

What famous phrase did John F. Kennedy say in his 1963 speech at the Berlin Wall?

Ich bin ein Berliner (I am a Berliner)

, .

What states border Lake Erie?

Michigan, Ohio, Pennsylvania and New York and the Canadian province of Ontario

, .

What was not considered an alcoholic drink in Russia until 2011?

Beer. Previously it was sold as a soft drink.

, .

What author was best known for his 1926 Weird Tales entry "The Call of Cthulhu"?

H.P. Lovecraft

, .

What is Europe's largest Ferris wheel called?

The London Eye

, .

What does the last place finisher of the Iditarod Sled Dog race get?

A red lantern

, .

What tech company launched a clothing line in 1986?

Apple

, .

There are how many cars in use in the world today?

Over 1 billion cars

, .

What did John F. Kennedy do with his salary as congressman, and later as U.S. President?

With plenty inheritance from his family fortune, he donated his entire salary to various charities.

, .

Are there mice in the London Underground?

Almost half a million mice live in the London Underground.

, .

What was Smokey the Bear based on?

An orphan bear found in a wildfire in New Mexico

, .

Though it's advertised as "Australian for lager", where is Foster's beer brewed?

Britain

, .

How many sharks are killed by humans every year?

100 million sharks

, .

Why is the Oakland Athletics mascot an elephant?

In 1902, the team was called "a white elephant", whose cost exceeded its value. The new owner Connie Mack then adopted a white elephant as the team's logo.

, .

What is the estimated amount of food thrown out in America each year?

Over 35 million tons of food

, .

When Libyan leader Muammar Gaddafi's compound was raided, rebels found a photo album filled with pictures of whom?

U.S. Secretary of State Condoleezza Rice

, .

What was the first clothing line featuring the Calvin Klein brand name?

Women's coats

, .

What country's Easter celebration includes swallowing a willow catkin from a branch?

Poland

, .

During the middle ages, larger birds were used to prey upon smaller birds such as quail in what activity?

Falconry

What is Diet Coke sweetened with?

An artificial sweetener called aspartame

, .

What is the best-selling book of all-time?

Don Quixote

, .

What essential cookie ingredient was invented in 1937 by Ruth Graves Wakefield of the Toll House Inn?

Chocolate chips

, .

Tom Kenny is best known for his work as the voice of what cartoon character?

SpongeBob SquarePants

, .

How many Christian denominations are there worldwide?

Over 33,000 denominations

, .

What building in Minnesota has never had central heating?

Mall of America

، •

How many Americans watch TV while eating dinner?

40% of Americans

، •

What generic work task marketplace is owned by Amazon?

Mechanical Turk

، •

During Hanukkah, how many candles are lit throughout the entire 8-day celebration?

44 candles

،،

How many escalators are there in the state of Wyoming?

Two

، •

What was the last film rented from
Blockbuster Video?

This is the End

, .

During Mardi Gras in New Orleans who must
wear a mask at all times?

Float riders

, .

When was Lyme disease first identified?

1975, in Old Lyme, Connecticut

, .

In cricket, what does the term "home run"
mean?

*A home run in cricket means the runs are
automatically scored if the ball touches or lands over
the boundary.*

, .

How many genes are in a human?

There are around 24,000 genes in human bodies.

, .

What player was still paid $4 million for playing basketball when he tried out for the Chicago White Sox baseball team in 1994?

Michael Jordan

, .

How many students drop out of high school in the U.S. every year?

Over 1.2 million students

, .

What olympic athlete is known as the "World's Fastest Man"?

Usain Bolt. He has beaten his own 100 meter records twice.

, .

What college football team was originally called "the Trinity Eleven"?

Duke Blue Devils

, .

Who became the oldest man to win swimming gold at the 2016 Summer Olympics?

Michael Phelps. This record was originally set in 1920.

, .

hat creature eats with tube feet which surround their mouths?

Sea cucumbers

, •

Whose dog was banned from Camp David after attacking President Bush's dog?

Dick Cheney's dog, Barney.

, •

When was the last olympic games to include gold medals which were actually made of gold?

1912 Summer Olympic Games, Stockholm, Sweden

, •

What was the first form of life on Earth?

Bacteria

, •

What inspired Kansas Chiefs owner Lamar Hunt in naming the Super Bowl?

His daughter's new toy Super Ball

, •

What boxer knocked out Mike Tyson in 1990 to win the undisputed heavyweight title?

James "Buster" Douglas

, .

What did Clinton officials do to over 100 computer keyboards in the White House before George W. Bush took office?

They removed the 'W' key.

, .

How did the "X-Y position indicator for a display system" get nicknamed the mouse?

Because the 'tail' came out the end.

, .

What is PEZ candy named after?

It is named after the German word for peppermint, Pfefferminz.

, .

Before his successful singing career, what did Julio Iglesias do professionally?

He was a goalkeeper for Real Madrid Castilla

, .

Between 1900 and 1920 what contest was actually an Olympic sport?

Tug of War

, .

What is the most isolated group of islands on Earth?

Hawaii

, .

What sport was the only Olympic event to ever involve motors?

Water motorsports, 1908 Summer Olympics

, .

What were the "fireside chats"?

A series of radio addresses by President Franklin D. Roosevelt between 1933 and 1944.

, .

What U.S. president owned a pet raccoon, which was meant to be eaten for Thanksgiving dinner?

Calvin Coolidge

, .

How much atmospheric pressure weighs humans down?

One ton

, •

Egg yolk is used to mix color pigments in what type of paint?

Tempera

, •

How tall are the White Cliffs of Dover?

Over 300 feet high in some areas

, •

What is the smallest bat in the world?

Bumblebee bat

, •

Who were the first father-son duo to hit back-to-back home runs?

Ken Griffey Jr. and Ken Griffey Sr.

, •

What color was Oscar the Grouch during the first season of "Sesame Street"?

Orange

, .

What is the age limit to cross the U.S. Canadian border alone?

People 17 and younger must be accompanied by an adult who is 18 or older

, .

Why is the Alabama vs. Auburn college football game called the Iron Bowl?

Birmingham, Alabama's role in the steel industry

, .

Is 'happy cabbage' a type of vegetable?

Happy cabbage is defined as a sizeable amount of money to be spent on self-satisfying things. (The Dictionary of American Slang)

, .

What future U.S. President was once Stanford University's football team manager?

Herbert Hoover

, .

Who was the first edible ice cream cone created by?

By Ernest Hamwi at the 1904 St. Louis World's Fair with a rolled waffle.

, .

What moon in our solar system has active volcanoes?

Io, a moon of Jupiter

, .

What was U2 singer Bono's birth name?

Bono was born Paul David Hewson.

, .

Who named the state of Florida?

Spanish explorer Juan Ponce de Leon named it La Florida ("land of flowers")

, .

In 2013, how did the military get rid of the brown tree snakes on Guam?

They dumped 2,000 dead acetaminophen dosed mice on the forest, which the snakes ate and died.

, .

How fast is the New York subway?

About 55 mph, but rarely travel over 30 mph

, ·

What is the full name of the Statue of Liberty?

Liberty Enlightening the World

, ·

Where was the first human case of HIV?

Researchers believe it was in Kinshasa, Congo in 1920

, ·

What is the population of California?

About 39 million

, ·

What was Hawaiian Punch originally used for?

It was originally developed in 1934 as a tropical flavored ice cream topping.

, ·

Where is the largest colony of bats in the world?

Bracken Cave, Texas

How long does human ossification take?

It takes 25 years for all bones to completely form.

, .

How many albums has the rock band KISS sold?

Over 100 million albums worldwide

, .

What makes hockey pucks glide so smooth and fast?

All NHL pucks are frozen before games.

, .

General Simon Bolívar y Palacios was the first president of what country?

Colombia

, .

What popular song was Thurl Ravenscroft best known for?

You're a Mean One, Mr. Grinch

, .

What is the oldest living tree in the world?

A bristlecone pine in the White Mountains of California (4,841 years old)

, .

What do the HB rings do that no other wedding ring does?

Through a smartphone app, your heart beat can be felt by your loved one.

, .

Who was homeless in the late 1980s before becoming a comedian?

Steve Harvey

, .

What state was once the largest producer of toothpicks in the United States?

Maine. The last toothpick plant in Maine closed in 2003.

, .

What is the vortex flame researchers have found that could help clean up oil spills?

Blue whirl

, .

What is featured on the Wyoming
state license plate?

A man on a bucking bronco

, •

It took eight hours to apply Ryan Reynolds' full
body makeup for what action film?

Deadpool

, •

From the 'Harry Potter' series: what does the
Hogwarts motto, "Draco dormiens nunquam
titillandus" mean?

Never tickle a sleeping dragon

, •

Who has the most wins among active
NASCAR drivers at Atlanta Motor Speedway?

Bobby Labonte (6 wins)

, •

After their Super Bowl XXI victory in 1987,
what team dumped a bucket of popcorn on
President Ronald Reagan at the White House?

New York Giants

, •

What apple variety was developed at the
University of Minnesota in 1960?

Honeycrisp apple

, .

When FIFA was founded in 1904, how many
countries were members?

*Seven. (France, Belgium, Denmark, the Netherlands,
Spain, Sweden and Switzerland.)*

, .

Why were people in Victorian London paid to
collect dog feces?

It was used to tan leather

, .

Who was the longest running Egyptian
pharaoh?

Pepi II Neferkare (About 62 years)

, .

What are the longest possible words
in a standard game of Boggle?

*The longest words that can be formed are
inconsequentially, quadricentennials, and
sesquicentennials.*

What song was banned by the BBC during World War II because it made factory workers clap too much?

Deep in the Heart of Texas

, .

What was the highest possible scoring word in Scrabble tournament play?

Oxyphenbutazone, 1,780 points

, .

What was Dr. Stanley Biber of Trinidad, Colorado best known for?

He performed 65% of the world's sex change operations from 1969-2003.

, .

What percentage of marriages in 2016 started on a dating website?

17 %

, .

What actor formed a Velvet Underground cover band called Pizza Underground?

Macaulay Culkin

, .

How many tons of electronics are disposed of worldwide each year?

20-50 million metric tons of e-waste

, .

Who wrote the song "Happy Birthday to You"?

Mildred and Patty Hill, Louisville Kentucky

, .

Where was the first test tube baby born?

Louise Joy Brown was born in Oldham, England in 1978.

, .

What December holiday was created on the television series "The O.C."?

Christmakkuh

, .

Who was the youngest person to portray Spider-Man/Peter Parker on screen?

Tom Holland. In "Captain America: Civil War" he was 19.

, .

How many people in the world
are infected with HIV/AIDS?

Over 36 million

, .

What item from "Saturday Night Fever" was
sold at an auction by movie critic Gene Siskel
for $145,000?

The white polyester suit worn by John Travolta

, .

Where did the word "breakfast" come from?

*It means to break a 'fasting' period of the prior night.
The term first described a morning meal in the 15th
century.*

, .

Who was known to wear an 'Oregon boot'?

*Prisoners of the original Oregon State Penitentiary. It
was a 28-pound ankle ring that kept inmates
from running.*

, .

What is the only state that grows
coffee in the U.S.?

Hawaii

, .

In 1983, what was declared the state crustacean of Louisiana?

Crawfish

, .

What U.S. state has the highest household income?

Maryland

, .

Most of what U.S. state does not follow Daylight Savings Time?

Arizona. The Navajo Nation lands observe daylight savings time since it spans across three states, Arizona, New Mexico, and Utah.

, .

What future criminal was a summer camp counselor at YMCA in the 1970s?

Mark David Chapman, who shot and killed John Lennon in 1980.

, .

What series began on NBC directly after Super Bowl XVII in 1983?

A-Team

What singer/actress started National Tree Day in Australia, responsible for planting more than 10 million trees?

Olivia Newton-John

، •

When is the animated film "Finding Dory" set?

One year after "Finding Nemo" (2003)

، •

What percentage of serial killers were bed-wetters?

Over 60% of serial killers were still wetting their beds as teenagers

، •

How big was the first 1 GB hard drive introduced by IBM in 1980?

It was the size of a refrigerator and weighed about 500 pounds

، •

What baseball player did George H W Bush meet while attending Yale University?

Babe Ruth

، •

Who discontinued their Noid mascot after a deranged man named Kenneth Noid held the restaurant's staff hostage after he thought the ads were about him?

Domino's Pizza

, ·

Who refused the best actor Academy Award for their role in "Patton"?

George C. Scott

, ·

What professional tennis player was eliminated in week 1 of season 14 of "Dancing with the Stars"?

Martina Navratilova

, ·

What broke the record as loudest NFL stadium crating 142.2 decibels of noise in 2014?

Arrowhead Stadium, Kansas City, Kansas

, ·

What WWE hall of famer's original ring name was Flex Kavana?

Dwayne "The Rock" Johnson

Astronauts on the International Space Station are at the same altitude as what visual phenomena?

Aurora Borealis

, .

What is the oldest continuously-operated motor racing circuit in the world?

The Milwaukee Mile

, .

What phrase appears on North Dakota license plates?

The Peace Garden State

, .

In 1804, where did the Lewis and Clark Expedition begin?

St. Louis, Missouri

, .

Why was Ken Mattingly replaced on the Apollo 13 mission?

Exposure to German measles (which he never contacted)

, .

How much does an average car weigh?

About 4,000 pounds

, .

What country has the most feral camels in the world?

Australia

, .

How did Bernie Madoff start his investment firm?

He saved $5,000 from working as a lifeguard

, .

How many people die from cholera every year?

About 142,000 per year worldwide

, .

What students in U.S. schools are suspended more often, black or white?

Black students are suspended four times more than white children

, .

When its founders found their search engine was a waste of time, what company was Google offered to for $1 million in 1999?

Excite

, .

What was built first, Stonehenge or the Egyptian Pyramids?

Stonehenge was built at least 300 years before the Pyramids.

, .

What company was originally known as Blue Ribbon Sports and operated as a distributor for Japanese shoe maker ASICS?

NIKE

, .

Who was the only single, unmarried president?

James Buchanan, Jr.

, .

Former Los Angeles Lakers star Earvin "Magic" Johnson is part of a group that acquired what baseball team in 2012?

They acquired the Los Angeles Dodgers team for $2.15 billion.

In 2010, Julian Assange founded what website site known for posting secret documents and emails?

WikiLeaks

, .

Who was fired from his first job for attempting to wheelie a bulldozer?

Evil Knievel

, .

How much do U.S. 'Big Brother' contestants get paid, whether they win or not?

Each houseguest gets $750 for every week they are in the house

, .

Tornio Golf Club is located in what two countries?

9 holes are in Finland, and the other 9 are in Sweden

, .

How many Japanese people are aged 100 or older?

Over 60,000

, .

Over 500,000 Buddha statues
can be found where?

Thanboddhay Pagoda

, .

Who caused a mass execution of cats in the
13th Century, which some believed led to the
spread of the black plague, caused by rats?

Pope Gregory IX

, .

What did some breweries do in Japan to
prevent blind people from accidentally buying
beer?

*Stamping the word "ALCOHOL" in braille on the tops of
their cans*

, .

Who could join the Roman Army?

Only men, at least age 20.

, .

How fast is Japan's bullet train?

The record speed is 375 mph (603 km/h)

, .

The fox is part of what mammal family?

The fox is part of family called Canidae, including wolves, coyotes, and domestic dogs.

, •

How long is a full day on the moon, from sunrise to sunrise?

About 30 Earth days

, •

What Hindu gathering is considered the largest religious pilgrimage in the world?

Kumbh Mela Festival

, •

North Korea's Juche calendar coincides with the birth of what leader?

Kim Il-sung (The year 2016= Juche 105)

, •

What country banned Buddhist monks from reincarnating without government permission?

China

, •

People can be prosecuted in 17 European countries for what criminal offense?

Holocaust denial

, ·

How much did Elvis Presley's family pay for Graceland in 1957?

$102,500

, ·

What product was patented by Canadian pharmacist Marcellus Edson in 1884?

Peanut Butter

, ·

What spread is better, butter or margarine?

Margarine, which is made from vegetable oils, and contains good fats which reduce bad cholesterol

, ·

Who planted a 500-acre corn field for the film "Interstellar"?

Director Christopher Nolan, who later sold the crop.

, ·

Out of over 7 billion people in the world, how many have access to working toilets?

About 4.5 billion people

, .

Who became the first police force in Australia?

Well-behaved convicts

, .

How many lakes are in Canada?

There are about 32,000 lakes larger than 3 square km

, .

What was the last film of actor Paul Newman?

Cars (2006)

, .

In 2012, what limited edition product was released by Pizza Hut of Canada?

Pizza Hut perfume

, .

What king was embalmed in a coffin filled with honey?

Alexander the Great

, .

What did the Pentagon prohibit the use of in 2001?

Chinese-made black berets for American Army soldiers

, .

It is a legal requirement to do what at all times in Milan, Italy?

Smile at all times except in hospitals or funerals.

, .

What is the only fruit with seeds on the outside?

Strawberry There's about 200 seeds on an average strawberry.

, .

How many pandas are in the United States?

There are 12 giant pandas in captivity in the U.S.

, .

Where is the Bermuda Triangle located?

It is in the western part of the North Atlantic Ocean

, .

What was Martin Luther's profession when he started the Protestant Reformation?

A German monk

, .

In the 18th century, what was platinum also known as?

White gold

, .

A geological phenomenon called sliding rocks occurs most notably in what location?

Racetrack Playa, Death Valley, California

, .

What large plant-eating dinosaur was discovered in Patagonia in 2005?

Dreadnoughtus

, .

What neurotransmitter spikes when you kiss someone the first time, craving more?

Dopamine

, ·

What does the Rainbow Foundation of Amsterdam pay alcoholics for cleaning the city streets?

10 Euros, half a packet of rolling tobacco and 5 beers

, ·

All people with what color eyes share one common ancestor?

Blue. Originally, people only had brown eyes.

, ·

A 32-foot tall effigy of Michael Jackson is located where in the Netherlands?

A McDonald's restaurant in Eindhoven, Netherlands.

, ·

What country has a strategic maple syrup reserve?

Canada

, ·

What is the world's smallest dolphin species?

Maui's dolphin

, .

What did two filmmakers create in the Black Rock Desert of Nevada?

A scale model of the Solar System

, .

Who hosted the reality show called "Mr. Personality"?

Monica Lewinsky

, .

Other than an IMAX theater, there are no cinemas in what country?

Saudi Arabia

, .

How long can people live without sleeping?

264 hours (about 11 days)

, .

How long does it take for your brain
to react to alcohol?

It takes 6 minutes

, .

China retains all ownership of what animal
throughout the world?

Giant Panda

, .

What city has installed 'smart palm trees'
enabling beach goers unlimited wifi on their
mobile phones?

Dubai, United Arab Emirates

, .

What scientific method makes painkillers out
of venom?

Toxineering

, .

What percentage of the world's
animals are insects?

80% of all animals are insects

, .

Where does most of Norway's electricity come from?

98% is from hydroelectric plants

, .

Who was known as "the fifth Beatle"?

Original bass player Stuart Sutcliffe

, .

What is the uncommon feature of the Cerbera odollam tree, found in India?

Known as the suicide tree, the fruit's seeds are highly toxic and are used to produce rat poison.

, .

When do male elephants leave their herd?

At about age 12, and they become solitary, moving to different herds

, .

Why might some people fear the pope?

They may have Papaphobia, fear of the pope, or the Roman Catholic church.

, .

What currency is not accepted on overseas U.S. military bases, to spare shipping costs?

Pennies.

, .

How many species of bears are there?

Eight species. Black bear, Brown bear, Polar bear, Asiatic black bear, Andean bear, Panda bear, Sloth bear, Sun bear

, .

Which former U.S. president created the political cartoon called "Join, or Die"?

Benjamin Franklin

, .

How many Americans served in World War I?

4,734,992 Americans. The last American World War I veteran died in 2011.

, .

What is the largest American Indian population of all the Native American reservations?

Navajo Nation

, .

Well known for hanging women during the Salem Witch trials, Reverend Cotton Mather preached about what Puritan belief?

The Rapture

, .

If someone weighs 150 pounds on Earth, they would weigh how much on the moon?

They would weigh about 25 pounds on the moon. Weight on the moon is about one-sixth what it is on Earth.

, .

Why do blonde-haired people get skin cancer quicker?

Blondes produce less melanin, so their skin more susceptible to skin cancer.

, .

What is the fastest growing demographic on Facebook?

Women aged 55 or older

, .

Who was named honorary chief by the Mohawk Nation because of his work in translating and documenting their language?

Alexander Graham Bell

Between 1947 and 1969, 12,618 UFO sightings were reported to what agency that was headquartered at Wright-Patterson Air Force Base, Ohio?

Project Blue Book

, .

People are born with what fears?

Fear of falling and loud noises

, .

Cigarettes are smoked by how many people worldwide?

Over 1 billion people smoke cigarettes.

, .

What author's works are the most heavily filmed?

William Shakespeare. Over 410 of his works have been either on either TV or feature films

, .

What is the lightest solid material?

"Aerogel" is the lightest solid material in the world.

, .

How tall was Mother Teresa?

Five feet tall

, ·

For an April Fool's joke in April 2000, what web search feature was announced by Google?

They announced the brain-scanning MentalPlex

, ·

Who drinks more alcohol, men or women?

Men are 69% more likely to report drinking alcohol than women

, ·

In medieval times, what were bras called?

Breast bags

, ·

What is the circumference of Earth at the equator?

24,901 miles (40,075 kilometers)

, ·

What dairy product did the U.S. Agriculture Department propose as a substitute for meat in school lunches in 1996?

Yogurt

What NFL teams have never played in the
Super Bowl?

*Cleveland Browns, Jacksonville Jaguars,
Detroit Lions and Houston Texans*

, .

What is the world's largest pyramid?

*The world's biggest pyramid is Great Pyramid
of Cholula, Mexico*

, .

How many steps does it take to walk one mile?

Average is about 2000 steps to walk 1 mile

, .

What word describes the meat of a deer?

Venison

, .

What is the average weight of a newborn baby?

About 8 pounds

, .

What actress nearly ruined her dresses while
on the set of "American Hustle" with stains
from Doritios?

Jennifer Lawrence

Almonds, apples, and peaches are part of what plant family?

Rosaceae (the rose family)

, .

What former military policy on gays and lesbians cost taxpayers over $500 million since it started in 1994?

Don't ask, don't tell

, .

How many calories are in one gram of fat?

There are 9 calories in 1 gram of fat

, .

The state of Alabama didn't lift its ban on what until 2000?

Interracial marriage was not legal in Alabama until 2000.

, .

Who was given an engagement ring when she was only two years old?

Queen Mary I

What Native American tribe assisted the Pilgrims for the harvest celebration today we call Thanksgiving?

The Wampanoag Confederacy

✦

What organization settled a lawsuit in 2002 with the World Wrestling Federation over the trademark "WWF"?

World Wildlife Fund. Since 2002, the company has been known as World Wrestling Entertainment Inc. (WWE).

✦

What is the only NFL team that does not have a helmet logo?

Cleveland Browns

✦

How far would you have to walk to burn off a single plain M&M chocolate candy?

The length of a football field

✦

A 17th century typographical error printing the King James Bible instructed readers to do what?

Thou shalt commit adultery. This error became known as The wicked bible.

In 2004, what company paid $33 million for a two-minute commercial featuring actress Nicole Kidman?

Chanel

, .

Almost the entire student body of what school enlisted in the Confederate army during the U.S. Civil War?

University of Mississippi. Only four students of 135 students returned from the war.

, .

In 1991, whose rendition of "The Star-Spangled Banner" reached number 20 on the Billboard Hot 100 chart?

Whitney Houston

, .

Where is the world's largest telescope?

The 500-metre Aperture Spherical Radio Telescope (FAST) is located in southwest China.

, .

What city was built on seven hills?

Rome, Italy

What percentage of adults worldwide have diabetes?

8.5% of adults

, .

What famous singer was born in 1947 with the name Reginald Dwight?

Elton John

, .

Who was the oldest person in the Bible?

Methuselah. He lived to age 969.

, .

Who was the only non-human to testify before the U.S. Congress?

Elmo, in defense of funding music programs in public schools

, .

What invention appeared in H.G. Wells' 1899 book "When the Sleeper Wakes"?

Automatic doors

, .

What is the fastest growing plant?

Bamboo. It grows up to 91 cm (35 in) per day

, .

What musician released an album titled "Song Reader" in 2012 which was only a book of sheet music and art?

Beck

, .

Who were the twelve Olympians of Greek mythology?

Zeus, Hera, Poseidon, Demeter, Athena, Apollo, Artemis, Ares, Aphrodite, Hephaestus, Hermes, and Dionysus

, .

How are fishermen reducing green sea turtle deaths?

They attach green LED lights to their nets

, .

What was originally designed as a temporary World's Fair exhibit, and was due to be

demolished in 1909 but became useful as an antenna in World War I?

Eiffel Tower

What rapper's real name is Armando Christian Pérez?

Pitbull

, .

In what year was the National Flag of Canada inaugurated?

The "Maple Leaf flag" was inaugurated on February 15, 1965.

, .

What is the currency of Hungary called?

Forint

, .

Best known for her role as Olivia Benson on the series "Law & Order: Special Victims Unit", Mariska Hargitay is what blonde bombshell's daughter?

Jayne Mansfield

, .

Who made her way into the Guinness Book of World Records as the 'most downloaded person of 1999'?

Cindy Margolis

What type of rock is Mount Rushmore carved from?

Granite

, ·

What author was born and died the same years that Halley's Comet flew past Earth?

Mark Twain (Samuel Clemens) He died one day after it appeared in 1910.

, ·

What was The Beatles' album "Abbey Road" originally going to be called?

Everest. The band did not wish to travel to the Himalayas for a photo session.

, ·

What popular wedding dance was created by accordion player Werner Thomas from Switzerland, in the 1950s?

Chicken Dance

, ·

How much water does the average human consume?

Humans drink about 16,000 gallons of water in their lifetime.

'Grand Theft Auto' was released primarily for what gaming console?

Sony Playstation

, .

Who is Arnold of Soissons known as?

The Catholic Saint of Beer (hop-pickers, beer brewing

, .

How long did the Roman–Persian Wars last?

The wars between Romans and Persians lasted about 721 years. It was the longest conflict in history.

, .

In what state is it illegal to push a live moose out of a moving airplane?

Alaska

, .

What was required for the American astronauts after they returned from the moon?

They were placed in quarantine

, •

Actress Molly Ringwald was in the original cast of what 1980s TV series?

The Facts of Life

, •

What is the second most commonly spoken language in the United States?

There are over 37 million native Spanish speakers

, •

What author said to cure writer's block he hangs himself upside down in his house?

Dan Brown

, •

How big was a stegosaurus' brain?

About the size of a walnut, no more than 80 g (2.8 oz)

, •

Forrest and LeRoy Raffel founded what restaurant in 1964?

Arby's

How often do Americans check their phones?

Collectively over 8 million times a day

/ .

What was Don Knotts' last theatrically released film?

Chicken Little (2005)

/ .

What headline did a Trenton, New Jersey print in 2002 when a mental hospital caught fire?

ROASTED NUTS

/ .

When is free Slurpee day at 7-Eleven?

July 11 (7/11)

/ .

Who sang the song "Freedom" for the first time, at Woodstock, making the words up as he played?

Richie Havens

What is the world's smallest ocean?

Arctic Ocean

What is the oldest city in the state of Wisconsin?

Green Bay, founded as a trading post in 1634.

The Battle of the Little Big Horn was included in what 1890 massacre?

Wounded Knee

In what year was the Great Wall of China completed?

206 BC

Who was the last King of the United Kingdom?

George VI, from 11 December 1936 until his death in 1952

What was Corey Feldman's character
in "The Goonies"?

*Mouth. Corey Haim also auditioned for the role. The
two later starred in six movies together.*

What reality star was banned from selling Girl
Scout Cookies?

*Honey Boo Boo. She was never an actual Scout, and
was selling signed boxes online.*

More Books by Bill O'Neill

THE BIG BOOK OF
RANDOM
FACTS...

BILL O'NEILL

Thanks for reading!
If you could leave a little review on this book on
Amazon.com that would be so helpful!

Thanks again
Bill O'Neill